Atonement

New Beginnings Series
Book 2

JM Dragon & Erin O'Reilly

Affinity E-Book Press NZ LTD

Atonement

2011 © JM Dragon & Erin O'Reilly

Affinity E-Book Press NZ LTD
Canterbury, New Zealand

ISBN-13: 978-0615581361
ISBN-10: 0615581366

Editor: Patty G. Henderson
Editor: Nancy Kaufman
Editor: Jo Atkins
Cover Design: Helen Hayes
Photo Credit: NASA Goddard

Acknowledgements

Thank you to all the women in the background who helped in bringing Atonement to this point. Nancy and Jo—you are the foundation that keeps us grounded and out of editing trouble. Gail and Patty thank you for your editing expertise. Helen, thank you for taking our vision of the book cover and bringing it to life.

Dedication

For Teresa Luis

Chapter One

The two women slept snuggled in each other's arms. The day was full of high emotion and great joy, making a good night's sleep necessary. The shrill ring of the phone startled them awake and Maggie answered. "This better be good."

"Maggie, I'm sorry to wake you but I need to speak with Lori immediately."

"Sure, Steve, just a minute. It's your dad."

Lauren took the receiver with a frown. "Hi, Daddy."

"Honey, your mother has taken a turn for the worse. She's in renal failure. I need you here."

"Damn. I was afraid of that. I'll be there in a few minutes," Lauren said.

Maggie was already out of bed getting their clothes together. "What's up, babe?"

"My mother took a turn for the worse. Dad needs me." Lauren took the offered clothes and quickly dressed. "You coming?"

"If you think it's okay. I don't want to be in the way." Maggie shrugged. "This is meant for only family."

"I need you with me, Maggie." Lauren held out her hand. "Don't you know that by now?" Lauren smiled when Maggie took her hand.

"Let's go then."

∞

They arrived at the hospital around three in the morning and found several locked doors before they entered through the emergency room. "I can't believe this," Lauren said. "Now we have to go all the way back to the front to find the elevator."

"Hey, relax," whispered Maggie.

Lauren turned and glared. "I am relaxed."

Maggie nodded. "The elevator is over there."

Tension filled the elevator cab for the short time they were in there. As the doors slid quietly open, Lauren saw her father waiting and she rushed into his open arms.

"Daddy, what did the doctor say? Does he know what the cause is? Can he help her?"

"Dr. Green is in with her now along with a specialist. We really don't know anything yet," Steve replied.

"I'm sure they will get her on dialysis as soon as possible," Lauren said. "I need to check on the tests for a transplant. Hopefully, I will be a good match."

"Sweetheart, we need to talk. Will you sit over here with me?" He put his arm around his daughter's shoulders and led her to the couch in the waiting room.

Once seated, Lauren patted the seat next to her and smiled at Maggie who duly sat down next to her.

"Right now, your mother is very ill and needs our support to get through this." Steve looked directly at Maggie. "You're included in this." With a fond smile, he reached over and patted Maggie's hand before turning his gaze to Lauren. "I have never been one to mince words with you and I won't start now." He took a deep breath.

"Just tell me what you have to say, Dad," Lauren said.

"As you know, your mother had a series of miscarriages before you came into our lives." Steve's lips tugged into a grimace. "The problem was with the fertilized eggs' inability to stay attached. We desperately wanted a child so we kept trying until it became obvious her health would be in jeopardy if we continued. At that time, there was experimentation with In Vitro fertilization and having money helped us. We found a woman who agreed to be a surrogate mother and she was implanted with the egg fertilized from your mother and myself. From the moment of your first breath your mother has been your mother in every way except for the actual birth." Steve took Lauren's left hand. "Do you understand what I'm saying Lori?"

Lauren sat there for several minutes digesting everything and squeezed Maggie's hand with her free one. *How lucky I am to have her in my life …my protector.* Her medical training told her all she needed to know about her chances of being a match and knew they wouldn't be any better than a random donor's would be. Yes, she shared her parent's DNA but her actual blood was from the surrogate. She looked first at Maggie and smiled before she turned to her father and gently touched his cheek. "If I can't save my mother, who will? A lifetime on dialysis is not the way for a vital woman like mother to live. We must find a way to help her."

"Sweetheart, we will find a way. Her name is on the national list of people needing kidneys. Right now, it's a waiting game. We won't lose her. I promise you that. If I have to spend every penny I have we will find a way." He hugged Lauren. "We can contact all her relatives and see if anyone is a match."

"What about Aunt Gloria? Surely by being mom's sister she would be a perfect match."

"Sweetheart, we haven't heard from Gloria in years. We don't even know where she is."

"I could ask my father to search for her," Maggie said. "He has the resources to find almost anyone."

"He's already tried, Maggie. Vicky's sister seems to have dropped off the face of the earth."

"You've already spoken with him tonight?" Maggie's brow furrowed. "You don't call him he calls you. What's going on here?"

Lauren saw the suspicion in Maggie's face and knew her dad had to gauge his words carefully. "No. No, not tonight. When the doctors first mentioned that this might happen I asked him if he could try and find her."

Maggie narrowed her gaze.

Lauren said, "Harriet. She's blood. She can help."

"Absolutely not!" Steve shook his head. "Your mother and I talked about that and she will not allow that to happen. She must want to see her mother. It cannot be out of pity but out of the bond between them. It's your mother's wish that she not know anything about her kidney failure." His eyes fixed on his daughter. "Do you understand that, Lori?" He watched as she nodded. "Good." His eyes tracked to the man coming their way. "There's Dr. Green. Let's go see what he has to say."

"I'll be there in a moment." Lauren turned to Maggie and wiped away an errant tear. "Finding her is imperative now. Will you help me?"

Maggie squeezed Lauren's hand. "Try and stop me." She gently stroked Lauren's face. "How do you feel about what your father just told you?"

"Told me? What do you mean?"

4

"About your mother not giving birth to you."

"Oh that." Lauren waved her hand. "I am her daughter in every way but birth."

"But…"

She touched Maggie's lips. "Shush. I don't love her any less. She wanted me and took a big chance at that time to give me life."

"But…"

Once again, Lauren touched Maggie's lips. "Please, let me finish. There are no buts or regrets, she is my mother and always has been. Right now, we need to get her stabilized. Then, once that is settled, we need to find Harriet Aristides."

"I'm right there with you. I'll use all the resources necessary to find her. I promise you that. Now, shall we see what the doctor has to say and then we can go see your mom."

Hand in hand, they walked to where Steve and the doctor were discussing Victoria Walker's future.

∞

A month had passed and Victoria stabilized enough to return to the ranch with a private nurse. Three times a week a helicopter arrived to take her back to the hospital for the long dialysis session. Once a week, Dr. Green and the specialist, Dr. Bentley, visited her at the ranch.

With the demise of the mayor and his plans, Steve took the land they donated and began building a twenty-bed hospital complete with emergency room, small surgical suite and a kidney center. The trips to and from the hospital were too much for his wife and he would do whatever was necessary to make her comfortable. Most of the people in the area were self-employed and therefore health insurance costs were at a premium. By transforming the name of his ranch into a corporation, he could offer affordable health insurance to the area residents that needed it. As a business matter, it made sense if his hospital was going to be successful. At the same time, he helped his neighbors and friends. He used his considerable fortune to lure two very experienced doctors to the area to staff the hospital along with his daughter. With the imminent retirement of Doc Wilson, the town would need a new general practitioner and Lori was a perfect candidate.

∞

Lauren had gone back to her home to settle matters at the research facility before tendering her resignation. With her house sold, she had all her possessions sent to Gyrfalcon, her new home, for Maggie to sort out. It would be interesting to see how their tastes would mesh once both their belongings were in the same house. As her SUV ate up the miles between her and the love of her life, the thoughts that traveled with her became clear. After she arrived at their new home, she and Maggie could concentrate on the best approach for meeting Harriet. Once that happened, she could start convincing her sister to get to know her mother and hopefully she would offer to help. Whatever happens, I will be glad to get to know my sister. It will be like a dream come true.

Chapter Two

Nicky returned to jungles of South America where her research scientist parent's home was, to explain her situation with Harry. They had been so happy to learn that after her last visit to the States was over, she would be working there with them. Now she would have to disappoint them once again with her latest news. The gift she had brought them from Harry, something of Abby's that they could cherish, they accepted with gratitude and much emotion.

Harry would have been embarrassed.

She really had intended to work with her parents but seeing Harry again, she knew that she would never go back permanently. After she confessed her love and Harry allowed her inside, the fates smiled on them, not to mention Abby. They were now committed to spending the rest of their lives together.

She thought she'd gone through the hard part with Harry at the cemetery visiting her sister's grave site. That was a piece of cake compared to the actual arrival at her lover's apartment. In many ways, it was a shrine to Abby. Nicky saw traces of her sister everywhere—particularly in the bedroom. Their moods shifted dramatically. Of course, they could have put it down to their overwhelming emotions, but the portrait of Abby staring down on them was a wonderful dampener on passionate emotions.

"You did say she approved, right?" Nicky tried to inject some humor into the pregnant pause that happened as soon as they entered the master bedroom in Harry's apartment. For a second, she was certain Harry looked at her as if she was an unwanted interloper in the home she had shared only with Abby.

Harriet's glance turned to the picture—and her lips curled into what Nicky could only describe as the unhappy clown expression. Then moments later, it changed and whatever dark cloud had descended, suddenly lifted.

"Yes, I did. Are you uncomfortable with the picture?"

Nicky wondered how she could be uncomfortable with a picture of her sister. It was a marvelous accolade to Abby, but at the same time, it was a reminder of lost love. How can we take the first steps toward a new future with that constant reminder staring down on us? "No. I guess I just never expected to see such a vivid sign of Abby's presence in the room. Call it foolishness on my part."

"Do you want me to dispose of the picture?"

"No. No, Harry, you loved her … we loved her. It's hard that's all." Nicky's eyelashes were wet with unshed tears.

"How about I collect a few personal possessions and we go to your place?"

Nicky's heartbeat raced as she realized the concession Harry gave her—she was willing to give up her old life and join her in a new one that they would forge together. She smiled happily at Harry and moved closer before she stroked a gentle finger down her cheek. "Darling, remember that I've given up the apartment. I've moved all my stuff. I was going to stay with Diane until my flight back to the interior."

A perplexed expression crossed Harry's face, obviously contemplating the situation, as Nicky would have expected. A brilliant smile replaced the dour look as she swung Nicky up into her arms. "I can't exactly go stay with Diane too, now can I? It would look rather strange if the boss turned up on her doorstep. I do know a rather wonderful intimate hotel that might suit us until we get a place of our own. Unless you think we are rushing …"

Nicky smothered Harry with wet kisses. "That sounds like a perfect plan."

∞

Nicky watched Harry carry another heavy box full of their belongings inside their new home. It was quite a different Harry to the one people generally saw, and far from the executive image. Hard physical labor and sweat were evident as the woman took up the manual side of moving into their new house. Except for her short visit to see her parents, they'd been together for six months. Life as far as she was concerned could only get better. "Hey want any help."

Harry grinned.

Yep better and better.

Their new home was a beautiful rambling four bedroom house on three acres waiting for her green thumbs. Or, that's what Harry had laughingly suggested when they had gone to see the property. It wasn't exactly true, as the professionally landscaped grounds had a beautiful pond with its own small bridge including a pagoda. Nicky fell in love with the property instantly and the joy she saw in Harry's eyes made her know it was the place for them. It was simply perfect, plenty of room for entertaining, a study for Harry and a marvelous area for her to grow all the flowers and plants she wished.

Harry walked out of the house grimy from the dust on several of the stored boxes. She looked happy and relaxed. *She's a little ripe, but we'll take care of that later—together.*

"I love you, did you know that?" Nicky asked.

"Well, I love you too." Harry looked over at the pile of boxes waiting to go inside. "Where do you want me now?"

"Oh that's easy, right here in my arms." The smoldering look, that always took Nicky's breath away, crossed Harry's eyes.

"You may regret saying that?"

"Never." Harry picked her up and kissed her thoroughly before kicking open the door. Nicky's senses drowned in the arms and passion of her lover as Harry divested them of their clothes before they made love for the first time in their new home.

Chapter Three

Maggie stood on the deck looking out over the town below. She spent all day sorting through Lauren's belongings that arrived the day before and hadn't a clue where to put everything. She pulled out her phone and pressed speed dial for the Walker residence. "Hi, Vicky, how are you doing today?"

Vicky chuckled. "I'm going stir crazy."

"Yeah, being laid-up is the pits. How about a change of scenery? I've all these boxes and furniture that Lauren sent and haven't a clue as what to do with them. I'd like to have something in place when she gets here. Do you think if I came to get you and the nurse, you could come up here and help me figure out all this furniture? I can't believe what a mess this place is."

"Maggie, wild horses won't keep me away. I'm going mad with being good."

Maggie noted that Vicky's voice sounded strained. "You sure it won't tire you out too much?"

"No. Staying here staring at the walls is too much. Helping you will be a pleasure."

"Okay. I will be there in about ten minutes. Wait 'till you see this place, Vicky. Lauren is going to faint when she gets here." A smile crossed her lips as she thought of her love walking through the door of their new home. Home … our home, how wonderful that sounds.

"Maggie, I'll have George drive us there. That way he can help move the furniture. In fact, I will bring Thomas too. It will feel good to know I can finally be of use to someone. Recuperating is for the birds."

"Sounds good to me. I can use all the help I can get. See you soon." Maggie hung up the phone and headed to the master bedroom. "We will decorate this together." Her mind wondered back to the weekend and the wonderful time she and Lauren had …

As the two women sat together snuggled in a lounge chair, they watched the setting sun from their new home. The huge red sun hung low in the sky as pinks and purples with a splattering of aquamarine filled in across the horizon.

"Maggie."

"Mm-hmm."

"The sky is beautiful tonight. Remember our first sunset together?" Lauren stroked her hands.

"Mmm-hmm."

A satisfied smile crossed Lauren's face.

"How can I ever forget that it was our first sunset in a lifetime together?" Maggie gently kissed the head resting on her chest.

"I've been thinking about how we should approach my sister."

"And?" Maggie kissed Lauren's nape.

"When I was reading the file your father gave you about Harriet, I noticed her company is developing a new drug. I went to school with one of the doctors who is on the team there. She was my roommate in college and we've kept in touch. That could be our in—the new drug they are developing might help in my research."

"You must have been reading my mind," Maggie said. "I was thinking your reputation will help us too.

You're continuing your research even though you're going into private practice right?"

"Yes. You already know that. What's your point?" Lauren turned her head to look up at her.

"Well, since you're not part of the research center at Johns Hopkins anymore, maybe you could use that as a way of getting in." Maggie winked. "You need funding and you can test their new drug."

"That could work. Do you think I should talk to my friend first or just make an appointment?"

"Who would you make the appointment with? Your friend?"

Lauren turned completely around. "No. I would make it with my sister."

Maggie shook her head. "Lauren, I think there's some sort of protocol you need to follow. You can't just go to the head of the company. There's no way they'd give you an appointment. You'd need some sort of referral or someone who can vouch for you. I think your friend is the best way to go."

"Don't you see this is where you come in? Your father can arrange a meeting, can't he?"

Maggie studied the beautiful face and knew she had no choice. "Of course he can. Do you want me to make the arrangements?"

Lauren's arms went around Maggie's neck as she kissed her. "Thank you, thank you. Yes, please set it up. At last I will meet my sister."

"I will ask my dad to set it up. You might want to alert your friend that you'll be there. If she's integral to the company it wouldn't hurt to enlist her support too." Maggie knew this wasn't about research or the new drug but about a much different discovery. From what she'd learned about Harriet Aristides, Lauren

will need every advantage if she was going to have any chance of getting through to the woman.

"My friend, Nicky, is in research and development. I'm not sure how much influence she has. I suspect not much." Lauren grinned. "Think you can call your dad now?"

Maggie couldn't keep herself from laughing. "Yes, my impatient love, I will call him now." She kissed Lauren soundly before she released her hold and went for the phone.

Chapter Four

Nicky swung open the door to Harriet's PA's office. By her expression, she knew she caught Sally by surprise.

"Hi, it's only ten thirty you usually come around at lunch have I missed a memo?" Sally Smith grinned.

Nicky smiled at Sally who had become a dear friend. She always made her feel welcome. "Is Harry free for two minutes? I need a word with her. I promise it'll be quick."

Sally leaned her head to one side before she smiled warmly. "I think for you, Harry will take a two minute break. Want to go inside?"

"Are you sure?"

"Hey, Nick, if she doesn't take a break for you—need I say more?"

Nicky confidently walked to the closed door and knocked. "Come in."

Nicky popped her head around the door and a dark head of hair poring over papers on a large desk greeted her. "Yes?"

"Can you spare me couple of minutes, Harry?"

The dark head came up quickly and Nicky's heart skipped a beat as she drowned for a few seconds in the lightening smile that crossed Harry's face.

"Yes. Yes, of course I can. You don't need to ask."

The door closed behind Nicky as she ventured further inside and stood on the other side of the desk.

"I was wondering if you might be free for lunch tomorrow."

"Tomorrow? Give me a second." Harry pressed a button. "Sally, what does my schedule look like around lunch time tomorrow?"

"You're to meet with the lawyers, but I can change that to a breakfast meeting."

"Okay, do it. I'll give you the details of my lunch plans in a little while." Harry disconnected, steepled her fingers and began tapping them together. "I'm all yours. Now tell me where, when, and are you buying?"

"I didn't think it'd be this easy," Nicky said.

Harry laughed. "I'll let you in on a secret—I'm only easy for you."

"I'm glad to hear that and yeah, I'm buying."

"Good, are we celebrating anything in particular?"

"My college roommate is coming into town and I want you to meet her. She's bringing a friend and I thought …"

Before Nicky could finish her sentence, Harry stood up, closed the gap between them, and wrapped her arms around her. "You thought right. I want to meet your friend and I get the added bonus of having lunch with my favorite girl."

Nicky looked up into the smiling face of her lover and felt Harry's gaze wash around her like the gentle lapping of waves on the shore. "I love you, you do know that right?"

"Yes. You show me your love every day."

"I haven't caused a problem in your schedule have I?" Nicky frowned. "I didn't think about that. We could always change it to dinner."

Harry gently moved a finger over the frown and shook her head.

"If you need me for anything Nicky I will change my schedule. You are more important than business." Harry bent her head and kissed her. "Only one drawback … I need to leave our bed early. That way, I can have lunch with you and your friend. And, if you like, we can have dinner out too."

"God, I don't deserve you, Harry."

"Sure you do," Harry's grin broadened.

Nicky basked in the glow of their love until the buzzer of the intercom interrupted them. "I promised Sally only taking up two minutes of your time."

"Really? I bet she didn't believe you."

Puzzled, Nicky pouted.

Harry laughed.

"I think she worries when she has to remind me about getting back to work when you are with me." Harry kissed her nose and then her lips before she reluctantly moved away "We will continue this later, okay?"

"Oh, yeah, later is good."

Harry grinned. "Can't wait.

Nicky left the office and saw Sally smiling at her. "Bye," she said.

Sally laughed. "See you later."

Chapter Five

The jet was on final approach to Bush Airport in Houston and Lauren sighed deeply in anticipation of the meeting with her sister the next day. She felt a hand touch hers and she looked over to see Maggie smiling.

"It'll be okay. I'll be with you all the way."

"I know. I'm just nervous, that's all. It's not every day you meet your sister for the first time."

"What do you think about picking up our rental car and heading to the Regency after we land? I made sure our room would be ready for an early arrival. We'll have almost two hours before we meet your friend for lunch. Why don't I run you a nice bubble bath and you can relax all your cares away for an hour. I have the lead on a wonderful restaurant for dinner or ... we could always have room service and watch the sunset."

"I like the sound of that but only if you will join me in the bath. I'll even wash your back." Lauren let the smile on her face become playful. "As to dinner, I can't think of anything lovelier than sharing a sunset with you." She took Maggie's hand and kissed it gently before leaning into her. "I love you, Margaret Sullivan, more than you probably will ever know."

∞

Lauren raced around the room trying to find just the right outfit. The luncheon date was set for twelve-thirty. If she didn't get her act together, they would be late and she certainly didn't want that.

"Sweetheart, slow down. You're making me dizzy. I think the dress you had on ten minutes ago is perfect. Why all the fuss? This is your friend not your sister."

"Maggie, she's our way in to see Harriet. She told me she was bringing her friend who is in the upper echelon of the company. I need to make a good impression if we're going to get in to see Harriet. Is that what you're wearing?"

Maggie scrunched up her face. "I thought this was what you wanted me to wear. Do you want me to change?"

"No, not now. We'll be late so that will have to do."

Hands went around Lauren's neck as Maggie placed a small gold heart necklace around it. "It will be okay. You look ravishing and everyone will love you just as I do. Well, not just as I do, but I know they'll love you."

"Oh, Maggie, this is beautiful, I love it." Lauren moved to a mirror and brought the necklace into view. She opened it to see pictures of Maggie and herself. "Thank you."

Maggie kissed her gently and held her close once again. "Now, take a deep breath and let's go downstairs to the restaurant. What do you say?" She then kissed her again before taking her hand as they went out the door.

∞

When they entered the restaurant, Lauren smiled when she saw her friend Nicky waving. "There she is, come on." She took Maggie's hand and dragged her quickly toward her longtime friend.

"Nicky!" she exclaimed. "It is so good to see you again."

The two women hugged and giggled, rejoicing in being together again.

"Lori, you look wonderful. I see love agrees with you. You must be Maggie." Nicky held out her hand to the taller woman.

"Yes, it's nice to meet you, Nicky."

"I am so glad you called, Lori. I can't wait to hear about your research. I hope the new drug will be of help to you."

Lauren was all smiles. Nicky had always been a wonderful free spirit and people instantly felt drawn to her honesty and sincerity. *I wonder what she will think once she finds out that my real reason for being here is to meet the president of the company who just happens to be my sister.* "Nicky, you look wonderful. It looks like you've been out in the sun. It looks good on you."

"We just bought a house with acres of garden and I'm taking full advantage of the sunny days. That's a lovely locket, Lori. Did someone special give it to you?"

A smile crossed Lauren's face as she reached up and touched the locket then glanced at Maggie. "Thank you. It was a gift from Maggie."

"Please sit down. Harry, the executive I told you about, should be here any time now. You said you wanted an intro into the company and Harry might be the one to talk with."

"I'm hoping I make a good enough impression that he'll arrange a visit with the company's president for me." Lauren could hardly contain the excitement she felt knowing that she was getting closer to her sister Harriet.

"Tell me, Maggie, what do you do or is the good doctor keeping you?" Nicky chuckled. "Of course, I mean that in the kindest of ways."

"I'm in land development. Right now, I'm between assignments so I took the opportunity to join Lauren on this trip. Now, it's your turn, Nicky, what's your friend's position in the company?"

Nicky's face lit up as she looked past Maggie.

Lauren turned to see what had Nicky beaming. At the entrance to the restaurant, was the most astonishing woman she'd ever seen. Two men dressed in business suits followed close behind her.

Lauren studied the three and decided that one must be the man meeting them for lunch and the other man was with the woman. She sucked in a breath hoping she would make a good enough impression with the man. He held her future with Harriet in his hands.

"Harry's here." Nicky waved in the direction of the three strangers entering the restaurant.

All three entrants looked in their direction. The two men smiled and the woman merely raised her eyebrows a fraction as they all began to walk forward into the dining room.

Lauren had never seen anyone who gave off such an air of power as the woman heading toward the table. Her mother always held a similar air, but she could not match this woman's aura. The men trailing behind her now looked insipid in her wake. Then it dawned on her why the woman's features were so familiar—she looked just like her mother. *Oh crap, it's Harriet. I know it is. What do I do now?* She let out a gasp as her heart trembled. When she felt

Maggie's hand squeeze hers, she turned and gave her lover a weak smile. She didn't know what to do or say but when Maggie gave her a wink she knew that her lover would take care of everything. No need to panic. Not yet anyway.

"Sorry I'm late, Nicky. I was unexpectedly detained."

Lauren saw blue ice-cold eyes scan the table but saw a thawing when they settled on Nicky.

"Lori, Maggie, this is Harry." Nicky grinned. "Harry, this is my good friend Lori Walker and her partner Maggie Sullivan."

"Pleased to meet you both. Any friend of Nicky's is a friend of mine."

Maggie cleared her throat. "Harry, it is good to meet you too."

Lauren offered her hand and gave the woman her most brilliant smile. "It's good to meet you, Harry. I'm sure you are very busy so I'm glad you were able to join us for lunch." Lauren recovered her composure and went into professional mode. No way did she want her sister to think she was a blathering idiot. She'd have to play it carefully and not tip her hand until she had a chance to meet with her privately. *Maybe this way she will get to know and like me before I drop my bombshell on her.*

From Lauren's point of view, lunch was for the most part easy going. Their conversation touched on both personal and work related topics with the two college roommates doing most of the talking.

"Please excuse me. I won't be long." Nicky stood, grinned, and headed toward the sign marked restrooms.

"Hey, wait up, Nicky," Lauren said.

Third wheel came to mind, as Harry twirled the stem of the solitary glass of wine she had allowed herself over lunch. She studied Maggie who sat across from her. *What is it about her that is so disconcerting? She appears well heeled and very intelligent but there's something seething beneath the surface.* Harry was certain the woman was sizing her up as if she could see through her. Her partner Lori, on the other hand, was quite charming and it was a pleasure to listen to her talk about her experiences. After some time, Harry decided the only way to get information would be to ask. "Maggie, exactly where do you work?"

Maggie, leveled her with what she concluded was a calculating glance.

"Right now I'm working from our home. With technology being as flexible as it is, I can do my work from almost anywhere. Mainly, I let my partners do all the leg work."

"Technology has its advantages," Harry said. "I wish my profession was that malleable. You're lucky that you have partners that will do that for you."

Maggie shrugged. "What exactly do you do, Harry?"

Harry considered the question carefully. A gut feeling told her this woman knew exactly what she did. Nicky wanted her to have a lower profile at lunch and that was exactly what she planned to do. *What Nicky feels and thinks is all that is important to me.* "I'm in administration."

Maggie raised her eyebrows. "Lots of people envy those of us in charge but they don't realize how long the days and nights are just making sure everything gets done."

Harry nodded in agreement. "I would rather deal with ten surly men than one crying woman." She let out a small laugh before Nicky, who had apparently appeared from nowhere, slapped her arm.

"Harry, what a thing to say."

"It's true, Nicky. With an angry person I know exactly what to do, but with a whining, crying woman, I haven't a clue," Maggie said

Lauren slapped her arm.

"Hey, I only speak the truth."

"Of course, we could always take them in our arms and give them some solace," Harry said

They both laughed.

"You two are incorrigible. Good thing we love you," Nicky said.

"Yes, you should both thank your lucky stars," Lauren agreed.

"I do, every minute of every day." Maggie smiled at Lauren. "I thank my lucky stars that you came into my lonely life."

After that, the ice was broken and the four women enjoyed an easy conversation over lunch.

∞

Once she glanced at her watch, Harry realized that she needed to get back to the office. She had an appointment in an hour with some unknown person that a friend of her uncle foisted on her. She placed a hand on Nicky's and smiled. "Nicky, I'm sorry. I hate to break this up, but I need to leave. I promised my uncle I would meet with his friend this afternoon.

That's why I was late … I was talking with my Uncle Harry about the meeting."

Nicky smiled and took her hand. "I know. I'm glad you could make it for most of the lunch. You'll only miss the coffee."

Harry touched the side of Nicky's cheek. "Coffee later then?"

"Absolutely. I'll see you later. Will you make dinner later?"

Harry grinned as she stood. "Yeah, I'll get rid of this person as soon as I can. I'm sure it's nothing important. The bill has already been paid so enjoy yourselves and relax."

"Hey, I thought I was paying for lunch," Nicky said.

"You can pay me back later." Harry wiggled her eyebrows.

"It was good to meet you, Harry," Lauren said. "I hope we can catch up with you again soon."

Harry's keen glance took in the woman. Nicky's longtime friend is genuinely pleased to be in my company. That thought made Harry relax her guard. Normally she would be relatively quiet and listened rather than partaking in the conversation. But not this time. At first, it was to please Nicky but after the first half-hour or so, she found it easy to be friends with Lori. Maggie wasn't as forthcoming but Harry reckoned she had the same problem she did—they were there for their respective partners.

"It was a pleasure to meet you both. Nicky and I discussed dinner later this evening and I would be delighted if you joined us. Houston has some really fine restaurants with 'Daniel's Palace' the best of the lot."

Nicky gave a snort. "Harry, that place is always fully booked months in advance, There is no chance of getting a table this evening."

Harry laughed as she bent down and placed a kiss on Nicky's cheek. "Leave it to me."

Nicky smiled and nodded. "Are you sure you'll be free? Maybe your meeting will go over. I'm sure your schedule must be in tatters after making time for lunch. Whatever will Sally say?"

Harry hugged Nicky a few seconds and released her. "Sally will say, 'thank God she's found a life'. To tell you the truth, I haven't a clue who I'm actually meeting. I didn't have time to go into much detail. I left that with Sally. However, I promise you that I'll be available for dinner. You can count on it."

"I'll hold you to that promise. Now go, before they page you."

"Ladies, see you later. Enjoy your day." Harry left with her mind again on business.

Chapter Six

Once Harry had left, Lauren smiled at her friend. "Did you ever think that we'd both decide to play for the same team, Nicky?"

Nicky smiled. "It isn't as much of a surprise as I thought it would be, Lori. Now that I think of it, I guess I always knew who attracted me … I just never thought too much about it." She shrugged. "I just did what was natural for me to do."

"Yeah, strange how that happens."

"She looks … well, fantastic comes to mind. How did you catch her?" Maggie asked.

Nicky stared at Maggie and the memory of a conversation she had with her parents pushed its way to her consciousness …

Eden Martin studied her youngest child as she talked animatedly with her father. David, her husband, never could comprehend what his daughter's nervous chatter meant. Nichola needed to tell them something and Eden had a feeling it wasn't going to be good news.

Her eyes settled on the large portrait that Nichola had brought with her, a present, she said, from Harriet Aristides. It was a beautiful piece and had captured Abby at her happiest. Eden speculated that she was probably thinking or looking at the woman who had commissioned the painting. As she went closer, she looked at the signature of the artist— S Parry. The talented portrait painter was unknown to her but she was certain that if the painting indicated the quality of their work, obscurity for the artist would soon be outdated.

"Mom, are you okay?"

Eden turned to her daughter and saw understanding in the clear depths of her eyes. *What a shame that Abby is no longer with us.* "Yes, you will have to thank Harriet for us. It's a marvelous portrait and it makes you think she's still here with us doesn't it?"

"I will be sure and thank her. She said it was painted the second summer she and Abby were together."

"The artist is very talented. Why don't you get him to do a portrait of you and Harry? That way we can have a family collection. I would really like to see that happen."

Eden watched Nicky solemnly stare at the canvas with tears threatening to fall. "I can't, Mom. Harry told me the artist died with Abby."

Eden closed her eyes as the tragedy of what happened hit her more profoundly than she expected. "I didn't know the name of the person who ... I'm so sorry. Harry must love you very much to give this up?"

"No problem, Mom. It's in the past and I need to look forward not backward. Harry believes I am her future and I intend to make sure she's right."

Eden placed a sympathetic arm around her daughter's small shoulders. "You best go sit with your dad. He's giving us one of those puppy dog looks he gets when he feels left out."

Nicky laughed softly as she stared at her dad.

Eden smiled lovingly at her husband who was looking at them with a hangdog expression.

"Mom I need to tell you that Harry and I are ..."

Eden hugged Nicky close. "I know, darling. Your dad and I expected as much. But we are glad you came in person to tell us."

"I love you, Mom."

Nicky let the memory go and smiled. "We caught each other," Nicky signaled for coffee.

A phone rang and Maggie pulled her cell out of her pocket. "It's my dad. I'll take it outside and be back shortly."

Lauren glanced Maggie.

"Is there a problem," Nicky asked.

"No, not really," Lauren replied. "I asked Maggie's dad to do me a favor hopefully he has good news."

∞

"Hi, do you have anything for me?" Maggie always made it her practice when using cell phones not to say too much or use names.

"I'll be meeting the party shortly and will have more information after that. I'll be in touch later."

The phone then went silent. So my dad is the person Harry is meeting. Huh, that's very interesting. I wonder why he's taking such a special interest in this especially now. I think it's time to do a little digging of my own. When she turned toward the dining area, she smiled as she saw Lauren heading her way with Nicky in tow.

"Nicky needs to get back to work and I would like to do some sightseeing. Want to join me?"

"At your service, m'lady. First, I would like to change into something lighter. It's hot out there and we did get that convertible you wanted."

"Lori, I'll call you later about what time we will pick you up for dinner," Nicky said. "Okay?"

"Great. Have a nice afternoon, Nicky. Bye."

The sexual charge emanating between the two women was unmistakable. Nicky shook her head and grinned before left the restaurant.

Chapter Seven

Harry drummed her fingers over the computer keyboard with her mind on several things. The keenest was the man who was due in her office shortly. Something told her he would be punctual and the conversation would be serious. As if on cue, the intercom sounded and Sally indicated her visitor was there.

All her senses were on full alert. She recognized that as indication of impending doom of some magnitude. *I've been here before and survived.* There was a knock on the door. "Enter." She stared at the opening door as the figure walked inside. The man was exactly how she pictured him, but taller, if that were possible. She was a good judge of character in most things and sized the man up carefully. His whole stance was quietly confident yet imposingly dangerous. His aura mesmerized her.

"Ms. Aristides, thank you for taking the time to see me."

She was sure that the softly spoken voice cloaked the steel beneath it. *He sounds like me when I am set to do battle in the boardroom.* She held out her hand and noted the strength behind his grip. "It's my pleasure, Mr. Resnik. Please, take a seat and tell me how I can help you."

The conversation was crisp and polite yet stilted as each evaluated the other while deciding the best approach. Their dance was like a prizefighter feeling out his opponent with soft blows, before making the final jab. However, Harriet felt that the man in front of her had the edge and she was damned if she knew how that happened. *This is my environment. Why am I letting him do this?*

"Good, a lady after my own heart. Immediate and to the point."

Harry inclined her head a fraction. "Is there any other way?"

The man chuckled and gave Harry a look. "No, not to my mind. I need you to make an appointment to see someone for me. It's very important."

She felt her brow crease and Harry fixed her gaze on the man. "Who and why?"

"Doctor L. V. Walker, she's in research and may have something to offer you. I believe you are always looking out for new possibilities?"

For a moment, Harriet was sure she had heard the name before. She normally could recall that type of thing instantly, but for some reason her mind went blank. *If she's in research, I probably saw her name in one of the journals. I will enquire as soon as this man leaves.* "Why would she offer her research to me?"

"That's not for me to say. She will want something in return and that is something only you can provide."

"I assume by that enigmatic comment, you will not provide me with any further information?"

Patrick Resnik traded glances with Harriet then shrugged. "You're right, I won't."

"One more question before you leave."

The man smiled and made an imperceptible nod.

"How come she needed you to make the meeting happen?"

"If she approached you, would you have seen her directly or would one of your underlings have been given the project to work on?" Patrick asked. "I take it that you don't personally supervise every idea that passes through your company's portfolio?"

"If I did, I'd be dead in a month. Do you have any idea how many projects we have currently?"

"I know precisely, which is why I decided to ask you personally."

"If you knew that, then what made you think I'd help you?" Harriet arched an eyebrow in question.

"Ah, my dear, Ms. Aristides, you said one more question not two. Perhaps you can ask again at another time." He passed a card across the polished desk. "I take it you will contact this number and arrange a meeting personally with Doctor Walker."

Harriet saw the small white business card with the doctor's name and phone number in a precise script that matched the man who stood before her. "Of course I will, for you have me intrigued."

"Ms. Aristides, once more, I'd like to thank you for your time." Patrick Resnik stood and left her office as quietly as he entered.

Harry stood there looking at the closed door, wondering why she had been completely and utterly under his control. *That's never happened before in my life.* Harry felt disconcerted like a storm was brewing with the wheels set in motion and she had no option but to ride it out. *How did I let a stranger come into my office, tell me what to do and I agreed? I don't have a clue as to why.*

Harry walked out to the reception area. "Sally, call this number and ask for a Doctor L. V. Walker. Arrange a meeting with me for tomorrow morning."

"Harry, you have a full all day tomorrow. We rescheduled so you could have lunch and the meeting with Mr. Resnik." Sally shuffled the papers on her desk and picked up her diary.

"I know that. Just, make the call and find me the time. Ten minutes should be enough."

Chapter Eight

Maggie stretched as she opened her eyes, acutely aware of Lauren's absence. She lifted her head and saw her lover looking out the window. "Guess this day didn't quite go as you hoped. What do you say we go out for a sightseeing drive now?"

Lauren smiled as she turned her attention to Maggie. "This day went exactly as I hoped. You are the only sight I need to see and you have such a wonderful way of pointing out all the interesting spots." She winked and walked over to the bed and crawled on top of Maggie. "You can take me sightseeing anytime." Her kisses turned passionate.

Maggie returned the kiss with equal passion, wanting and needing more but Lauren pulled away.

Lauren tilted her head as a serious look crossed her face. "Why don't you call me Lori like everyone else? Lauren sounds so formal."

"You want a nickname? I can do that. Anything for you. What about snookums or honey bunch?"

"No, that's not what I mean. Just call me Lori, that's all."

"Oh no, that's not good enough." Maggie tried to contain the smile that threatened to erupt. "I think lover lips would suit you."

"No."

"No? Okay how about sweetie pie?" The smile begged for release.

"Maggie, I'm serious about this. Stop making jokes."

"No joke, lover. I want your nickname to be something special, something that just I can call you." She went silent for a moment appearing to be in deep thought. "I have it. Honey lips. That is perfect."

"Maggie, that is yucky. I can just see it now— you're sitting at a lovely restaurant and I walk in. Across the room, I hear your sweet voice call out, 'oh, honey lips, I'm over here'. No thank you, Lauren will do just fine."

Maggie laughed heartily. "Oh honey lips, come give me a kiss with those sweet tasting lips of yours."

Lauren bit Maggie's lip before she kissed her. "I love you, do you know that?"

"I had an idea but maybe you should show me just how much, honey lips." Maggie pulled Lauren in for another kiss, ready to continue their afternoon of love making, when the phone rang.

Lauren rolled off Maggie and onto the bed laughing. "You'd think we would know better and get a room without a phone." She picked up the receiver. "Hello."

"Yes, this is Doctor Walker. ... Yes, I can be there at eleven. ... I see. I would like more than ten minutes but I will take what I can get. ... Yes, I know she's a busy person. ... Okay. Thank you, Sally. I will see you then."

Lauren looked at Maggie as she hung up the phone. "I have an appointment to meet Harry."

"Cool."

"Guess your dad was able to convince her to meet me." She sucked in a deep breath. "Maggie, what do you think will happen when she finds out?"

"I'm not sure. Shock, I would think. After all, she hasn't any idea you exist and she has had no contact with your mother since birth." Maggie pulled Lauren closer and kissed her. "I'm not sure how she will react when she sees you enter her office. We met her at lunch and we'll be with her and Nicky for dinner tonight, so I imagine she will ask why you didn't tell her then." Maggie shrugged slightly. "I'm sure your charm will win her over."

"You are only saying that because you love me and don't want to see me hurt." Lauren shook her head then rested it on Maggie's shoulder. "This is really important to me, Maggie. I really don't know what I will do if she turns me away."

Maggie pulled the wonderful, tenderhearted woman close to her. "It will all work out, I promise you that. When you feel the world closing in on you, reach inside your heart, and find my love. It will keep you safe."

∞

"What's wrong baby?" Nicky made a face in an attempt to get Harry to smile. They were due to arrive at the hotel to pick up Lori and Maggie within the next few minutes. All through the twenty minute journey, Harry barely said more than a few sentences. She arrived home from the office late and gave Nicky a perfunctory kiss before taking a shower and changing into her evening clothes. There was barely enough time to get to the hotel on time.

"Nothing. Why do you ask?"

"No real reason," Nicky shrugged. "It's been a long time since you've been this quiet. When we first met you were quiet but that was more out of being a loner than antisocial." She recalled her first meeting in the boardroom with Harry and Seth Roland and grinned. "I was so intimidated by you."

"You were? I didn't know that. I thought you just didn't want to go."

"Well, there was that too. You can be imposing at times."

"I guess."

"Please tell me what's bothering you."

"I'm sorry, Nicky, I guess I am preoccupied with work. I promise I'll be attentive from now on." Harry smiled.

Nicky saw her halfhearted smile and knew that something was troubling Harry. "I'd rather you told me what the problem is. If it's not top secret maybe we can work it out together."

"I would if I knew what it was that was troubling me." Harry smiled. "I feel kind of disconcerted at the moment and I can't quite explain why."

"When you can, will you tell me?"

"You will be the first to know. I promise."

As their eyes met, sparks appeared from nowhere. "I'll hold you to that. I'm beginning to regret having a friend in town."

Harry chuckled as she pulled up at the hotel entrance. "Why?"

"Because the way I feel at the moment, company is the last thing I want." Nicky's mind flipped back to how she felt at lunch and the raw passion she saw mounting in her friends when she left them. *I wanted Harry then, anyway, anyhow and still do. Guess I'll have to wait until we get home.*

Harry laughed and placed her hands on Nicky's to still them. "We'll make it a short dinner and then you can show me how you feel."

Nicky snorted. "I wish. I know Lori can talk the hind legs of a donkey and before we know it, the hours pass by because everything she says is so damned interesting. I love her. At school, she was like a …"

Harry looked at Nicky closely. "Like a what?"

"A sister. Lori is like a sister. I guess for four years she was my family and although we have gone on to different careers and don't see each other as often, she always will be a sister to me."

"Well, if she's a sister to you, I'll be good and listen intently to everything she says. Maybe she will tell me some juicy gossip from your college days."

"Don't go there, Harry. You might regret it."

"Really?" Harry raised an eyebrow.

"Yes, really. And what about you? Didn't you have anyone close when you were in school? Would you have liked having a sister?"

Harry cocked her head slightly. "Close in college … not really … well maybe one or two."

"Oh, no, Harry, you can't leave it like that. I'll torture it out of you … later." She knew exactly what would do the trick, for exquisite pleasurable torture always did.

"Later, I'm definitely up for later."

"Okay, what about a sister?"

"I did years ago."Harry grinned. "Your friends are here."

"On time, great. What about now?"

"Now? Now I have you. Why would I want a sister? I have everything and more in you. A sister would be nothing more than an unwanted piece of personal baggage to me."

"There they are." Nicky rolled down her window. "Hi, get in and we will be off."

The door to the rear passenger side of the vehicle opened and after the two friends greeted each other and everyone was in the car, Harry took them, as promised, to Daniel's Palace for dinner.

Chapter Nine

Nicky stared out of the lab window, her mind definitely not on the test she was performing. No, it was firmly entrenched in the evening she and Harry had enjoyed with her friends and now, she believed Harry's friends as well. Harry was rather deep when it came to tipping her hand on the relationship side of things and she knew that first hand. Lori had been her witty self and she had joined in the ragging of both Harry and Maggie, as they were silent for the first part of the meal. Then Maggie joined the good natured ribbing and before she knew it, Harry was regaling them with her own college exploits. Only Harry would call being studious an exploit. Still, her lover tried to be part of the group for the rest of the evening and for that, Nicky was thankful.

After they had dropped the friends back at the hotel, the drive home was in silence as they both digested the heady emotional undercurrents of the night. Once home and inside the house, Harry swept Nicky up and carried her to the bedroom. Words went unspoken, as their raw passion and need communicated all either needed to know. For Nicky, the lovemaking more than made up for her frustration earlier in the day.

Her thoughts turned to the evening before when Lori hugged her and said she had never been happier. She thought the statement was rather odd. Lori told her when she called to tell her she was coming to Houston how sick her mother was so the *happier* comment was a surprise. But, Nicky noticed a definite upswing in her friend's mood since lunch and on reflection, she realized that the way her friend and Maggie interacted, the good mood had nothing to do with sightseeing. At least it's not the type that you tell your family and friends. The very thought made her grin broadly.

"Hate to interrupt such a wonderful daydream but I think the test needs your attention," Diane Leyman said.

"Oh, sorry, Di, I was just … yeah, okay, daydreaming." Nicky laughed and returned her attention to her bench and the test she was running.

"Do I need to ask about whom?"

Nicky shook her head as she felt her cheeks heat up. Harry was constantly in her thoughts, her blood, and the air she breathed. "I have friends visiting from out of town and we took them to Daniel's Palace last night."

"Wow. How was it? I heard that place is booked solid for months and you need a gold card to place your coat in the cloakroom."

"That's an exaggeration, Di. Harry must have contacts because she said it wouldn't be a problem and it wasn't. The food was fabulous, you must try it." Just the thought of the different dishes from the evening before made her stomach rumble.

The phone on her desk rang and Diane, giving her a long suffering smile, answered the call. Diane's eyes traveled to her young friend. "It's Sally Smith for you."

Nicky winked at her boss and grinned. "Hi, Sally, what can I do for you? … Sure give me the name and I'll look it up for her. … No problem. … Please say the title again, Sally … The Arthritis Mind

Connection you say? ... I don't need to research the author, Sally. She's a friend of mine. ... Harry met her yesterday. ... Okay, I think I will call her and tell her myself."

As Nicky hung up the phone, she looked thoughtfully at the memo pad where she wrote the title of the book. The author was none other than her good friend Lauren Walker. Sally told her that Lori had an appointment with Harry at any moment. Now why didn't Lori tell me she was meeting Harry? If Lori was desperate to see Harry, why didn't she just come out and ask me? Nicky knew something wasn't right and a feeling of betrayal beset her.

"Trouble?" Diane asked.

"No. At least I hope not. Do you know a research doctor named Walker, Lauren Walker, or maybe L.V. Walker?

Diane's brow creased. "Arthritis. Yeah, she was in Chicago at a convention I went to a couple of years ago. She presented on rheumatoid arthritis. I can remember being absolutely engrossed. She's young, brilliant, and very attractive."

"Well, she's meeting with Harry any time now."

"Oh, that'll be a nice catch for Harry. If she can get Walker on board, it will compliment what you are doing with the new drug." Diane gazed at Nicky. "Why the gloomy look?"

"Because I went to college with her and we were roommates. I thought we were good friends." Nicky shook her head. "She's the friend we went to dinner with last night."

"Even better. I'd say that her joining force with us is in the bag then, wouldn't you?"

"That's just it, Di. We went through the whole evening and she never once mentioned it to either of us."

"Do you mean Harry doesn't realize L. V. Walker is the friend from last evening?"

"Yeah, that about sums it up. Do you find that strange?"

Diane scrunched up her face. "I'd say highly suspicious. Although, she may not have wanted to mix business and friendship, or … she didn't know it was the Harriet Aristides."

"Well, we never did mention who she was, only that she was in administration. I'd better call Harry and tell her the news. I guess she won't be happy at the apparent underhanded way Lori has dealt with the situation."

"Just be careful before you jump to conclusions without hearing all sides, Nicky. That's one of the mantras of all good scientists … gather all the facts before making the judgment. Besides, maybe your friend forgot or had a good reason not to mention the meeting."

"Pull the other one, Di. Would you forget a meeting planned with Harry?"

"Point taken. I'll take care of the test and you can call the boss."

Nicky picked up the phone and dialed the direct line to Harry's office. *Something is going on. What can it be? Oh Harry, I am so sorry I introduced you to her if this upsets you.*

∞

A reassuring arm went around Lauren's shoulders. "Hey, it will all work out. Remember, I promised you that."

"I know but this is so important. What if she throws me out and doesn't give me a chance to explain? This has to work out so she will come back to Warwick and see our mother. I just know once she gets to know her, she will consider donating a kidney if she is compatible."

"Small steps, Lauren. First, you need to see her. Next, you need to get her to accept you and your mother. Then, you need to convince her to go to Warwick. There is a long road ahead of us. If we go down it together and draw strength from one another, we will make it to the end." Maggie smiled and kissed the brown hair.

"Do I look okay?"

"Beautiful as always. Come on, Lauren, this isn't like you to be so unsure of yourself. Why not get your confidence back and march right into her office, say what you have to, and let the cards fall where they may."

"That's a good idea. I don't know why I'm acting this way either. There's no reason to be afraid. I will walk into her office just as you said and tell her we are sisters. She might be shocked at first but she'll be happy because everyone wants to be part of a family. Right?" She gave Maggie a tight hug. "Shall we go and keep my appointment?"

"Yep, let's go. We can't delay the family reunion."

∞

Maggie stopped the car at the main administration building. "Want me to go with you?"

"No, I need to do this alone. Will you wait for me?"

"Of course. I'll park the car then sit in the lobby until you're done. How does that sound to you?"

Maggie's infectious smile caused Lauren's spirits to soar. "Wish me luck." Before opening the door, she leaned over and kissed Maggie. "I love you."

"Good luck. I love you too." Maggie watched as Lauren entered the building and disappeared from sight before moving the car to the parking lot.

∞

As Lauren walked into the spacious outer office, she noticed no one was there to greet her. She only had ten minutes for the meeting so she decided to find the office herself. She stood in front of the oak door with Harriet Aristides' nameplate and a sense of trepidation filled her mind and body. She closed her eyes and let a vision of Maggie fill her mind before she calmly knocked on the door before turning the knob to her future.

∞

Damn. Harry hated her schedule going to pieces, even if she had been the one to make the arrangements. Even though the mysterious man from the day before only suggested that she meet with the doctor, she felt an obligation to meet with the person. Who the hell is this Walker woman anyway? Okay, she has done some good work, according to the net, on arthritis research, but it was nothing so spectacular that it immediately jumped out at me. She hoped that Nicky would come up with something tangible as to why the woman wanted to see her personally.

It wasn't one particular remark that Resnik made that had irked her and preyed on her mind. It was everything about him. Nicky noticed her preoccupation. She had been truthful to Nicky in that she really didn't understand why she felt as she did. Today however, was different. She was the one who was in control. She'd allotted ten minutes for the woman and ten minutes was all she'd get.

She hadn't felt this annoyed since her meeting with Eric Lasser and his admission of duplicity regarding the Martin's drug discovery. Her normal practice would have involved the authorities, however, the Martins, particularly David, had pleaded that she deal with his old friend with leniency.

Her mind drifted to the conversation she'd had with Lasser the one and only time she'd seen him after the revelation …

"All I want to know, Eric, is why?" Harry paced the conference room like a panther ready to pounce on her prey.

The man puffed out his chest and tried to speak but failed miserably.

"Cat got your tongue?"

"If you're the cat then I'd say the answer to that is yes."

"Business is business, Eric. I know this kind of thing goes on and frankly, I've learned to deal with it. But you, you of all people, Eric. That's what I don't understand. For God's sake man, they were your friends. No, they were your family. How could you treat them that way?"

The normally confident and jolly man remained quiet and defeated in the chair he slumped into upon arriving in the office. "You wouldn't understand."

"Damn straight. Talk about an underhanded, double-dealing traitor, you fit the bill. That's only what you did to your friends. I haven't even mentioned the company aspect yet. What was it? Did Cole offer you more money?"

"Not more money, unlimited money. I was running out."

Harry sighed heavily and put a hand across her mouth to stop the expletive that begged for a voice. "No one has unlimited money, Eric, unless you captured a genie in a bottle and it gave you three wishes. Don't tell me Guy Cole turned into a genie?"

"I think this discussion is pointless, Harry ..."

"Oh, no you don't. Never, ever, call me Harry again, Eric. Only friends and loyal colleagues call me Harry. I can say without doubt, you are neither."

Tears welled up in the older man's eyes as he realized, perhaps for the first time, what a mess he had made of his life. "I never wanted to hurt anyone. Don't you see that?"

"Hurt? Don't talk to me of hurt. You haven't hurt me, Eric. You merely wounded my business pride and that I'll survive. Shouldn't you be thinking in terms of your friends David and Eden Martin, not to mention Nicky, who adored you? You willingly betrayed them by trying to sell their discovery to the highest bidder."

"I know. I know. I feel so bad about what I did. It was all a mistake. A foolish error by an old man.

Harry snickered. "Foolish? That is quite an understatement, Eric. A foolish mistake is when you take the wrong coat and not when you consciously try to bring a company down."

"What are you going to do to me? Call the police and have me arrested?"

Harry stopped in front of the man and glared at him. "That's exactly what I'd like to do to you. In my opinion, that's what you deserve. However, you still have friends, though God knows why, and they have asked me to be lenient with you."

The old man looked up at her. "Are you playing with me? Why would anyone want to help me after what I did? Who would ever trust me?"

Harry turned her back on him. She had no time for his kind. It reminded her of her parents who abandoned her so they could go off and see the world. Some people never know what the word responsibility means. "David Martin."

"David? After all I've done, he asked you to do that?"

"Yes. He must think you have redeeming qualities."

"You obviously don't. Why did you agree?"

"Not that I need to explain myself to you, of all people, Eric, but I understand about responsibility to my friends, my family, and to my loyal staff. Perhaps you might learn that one day and realize where your gambling has taken you. Now get out of my sight before I change my mind."

The pent up anger that conversation always caused, washed over her with the unsettling vengeance she came to associate with that event. The phone rang at the same time she heard a knock on her door. Where is Sally?

Harry clicked hands free and said, "Hello," just as the door to her office opened abruptly and a determined looking woman entered her office.

"Harry, the L. V. Walker is my friend Lori."

Harry couldn't believe it. In front of her was Nicky's friend Lori and on the phone Nicky said the very same name.

"I know you never expected to see me here, Harry, but I have a good reason," Lauren blurted out.

"It had better be!" Harry emitted a low growl realizing that for the first time since she'd met Nicky, someone had truly surprised her. She ignored the fact that her partner was on the other end of the line as she opened her mouth then shut it.

Lauren walked further into the office. "Harry, I'm your younger sister and I've come to take you home to our mother."

There were two voices echoing in the otherwise silent room. One was Harry's deep astonished growl of 'sister' and, the other a squeal from the phone as Nicky repeated the word, 'sister'.

"Yes, Harry, I'm your sister. Isn't that wonderful news?" Harry struggled with the concept and then her intelligent mind kicked in. *Nicky is on the phone and her friend is in my office saying something very stupid. It's a prank. Yeah, it's a prank, from their college days.*

"You set this up didn't you, Nick?"

"No, she didn't. It is true. I am your sister," Lauren replied."

Nicky said, "Don't bring me into this because I haven't a clue what's going on. Do you want me to come up to your office, Harry?"

"You have to believe me," Lauren said.

"I'll call you back in a few minutes, Nick, this won't take long." Harry disconnected the phone and immediately regretted her actions. Damn, I shouldn't have done that. Nicky deserves better of me.

Harry looked at the woman and had the distinct feeling there was more to the story. How incredible is this? "Why should I believe you? Just who the hell are you? Are you Lori, Nicky's friend, Doctor Walker, a respected researcher, or someone else? Just what kind of game are you playing? Is this some elaborate prank at my expense?" Harry's blood boiled as her anger grew. "Well, let me tell you, I hate this kind of subterfuge. Trust me when I say this isn't how I expect someone who claims to be Nicky's friend to behave."

"I am your sister and I'm not playing a game. I want to get to know you and you to know me. I thought we both felt that bond yesterday. Didn't you feel it, Harry? It's as if a part of you that was missing is now open to you. I felt it and I was sure you did too."

Harry laughed derisively. "You live in a fantasy land, Ms. Walker. You were Nicky's friend and I was indulging someone I love. That was all there was."

Lauren's shoulders slumped. "I don't believe you. It's there, I can feel it, and I know you do too. I know I'm right."

"Do we share the same blood?" Harry saw a look of horror on the woman's face

"We have the same mother but have different fathers."

Harry hadn't spent years watching people's reactions not to know when a comment hit home. This woman isn't a relative at all. What is she up to? "I don't believe you. What evidence do you have?"

"My mother's first name is Victoria and she was married to your father forty-one years ago. I'm sorry I don't recall his first name. After his death, she went back to her hometown and finished school. Her maiden name was Maxwell."

"Precisely, you don't know. Get out of my office and out of Nicky's life too. She doesn't deserve you fucking with her to get to me. If you continue down this path, you will regret it."

"I have her picture." Lauren rummaged in her bag. "Here, look for yourself. You will see she is your mother since you look just like her."

"Go to hell." Harry flung the offered the picture away. "Why should I believe you? Come to that, why the hell do I want to see a picture of the woman who abandoned me when I was a baby?"

"People change and she has. She regrets all the years that she wasted not knowing you, Harry. Please believe me. It's all true."

Harry looked at the woman who was now a stranger and her heart hardened. It was obvious that the woman only wanted to be part of a corporation that was going places. She used Nicky to get to me so she can use our money and resources for her own gain.

"Then let her come here and tell me herself," Harry growled.

"She can't."

"Really? Now there's a surprise."

"She was shot and is recuperating therefore travel at this time is impossible."

Eyebrows rose and Harry contemplated the comment. Is it true, has my mother been shot? Why would I care? She hasn't bothered with me in forty years. "How was this woman you call mother shot?"

"The mayor of our town shot her when she refused to knuckle under to his blackmail."

The intercom buzzed and automatically Harry answered. "Yes."

"Your next meeting starts in five minutes."

"Thank you, Sally." Harry glanced up and saw the torment and sadness etched into the other woman's face. "Sorry, I need to be elsewhere. Perhaps we can chat about this another time." Harry's lip curled into a snarl.

"You can't leave it like this. Please look at her picture, please." Lauren placed the photo on Harry's desk.

"I have another appointment. I gave you ten minutes and you've taken," she looked at her watch, "fifteen. Be grateful I haven't charged you for my time. Goodbye, Ms. Walker. I'd love to say it was a pleasure, but alas, that's the last thing I would say to you."

Harry folded her arms across her chest as Lauren Walker's voice began to tremble and rise in pitch. "No. I will not allow you to dismiss me like that. What am I going to do? How can I make you understand?"

Unable to stop herself, Harry smiled at the woman and shrugged. "Beats me. Then again, I really couldn't care less. If you will excuse me, I have a more pressing engagement."

"What the hell is the matter with you? Is your heart made of ice? This is your mother we are talking about and not some stranger."

Harry's head turned in aggravation. "Lady, it is true that I have a biological mother. Was she a mother who loved me enough to stay around and care for me when I was sick or when I needed encouragement?

Was she there when I needed guidance as a young woman? Let me tell you, I have no one that covers that bill. But you do, don't you?"

Harry walk past this imposter and out of the office. "Don't be here when I get back because security will happily escort you from my building in a most undignified way."

Chapter Ten

Maggie walked quickly over to Lauren who seemed shocked and disoriented as she exited the elevator. "Lauren, what's the matter?"

Lauren looked at the woman speaking to her, as if she were a stranger before she collapsed, sobbing into her arms. "Oh, Maggie, she hates me."

"Shh, come over here and tell me all about it." She led them over to a couch in the lobby. "Here, sit down."

Lauren buried her face in Maggie's shoulder and continued to sob. "I need to be alone for a little while to sort this all out."

"Sweetheart, why don't we go back to the hotel and I will run you a nice hot bath then we can talk all about what happened with Harriet."

She stood and began to walk away when Maggie's hand stopped her. "Please let go of me. I need to be alone. Can you understand that?"

Maggie saw the vacant eyes looking down at her. "I can't let you go like this. How will you get back to the hotel? Where will you go? You don't know this town, Lauren."

"I think I'm old enough to find my way around. Now, if you don't mind, let go of my hand."

Shocked, Maggie watched as Lauren left the building. This isn't right, something is wrong. I can't let her wander around alone. Maggie headed for the revolving door and went outside ready to run to catch up with Lauren. What she found was nothing. In the blink of an eye, Lauren was nowhere. Fear gripped her heart as she stopped a man who was entering the building. "Excuse me, did you see a small beautiful woman with brown hair and eyes, just come out the door?"

"A woman got in my cab when I got out."

"What's the name of the cab company? I need the name."

"I don't know, lady. Look, I need to go or I will be late for my meeting."

Maggie searched the road for signs of the long departed cab.

I need answers and I need them now. She turned and stormed back into the building to find the only person that had the answers.

∞

Maggie didn't waste time when the elevator doors opened and hurried toward what she assumed to be Harriet's office.

"May I help you?" a woman asked.

"I need to speak with Aristides."

"She can't be disturbed at the moment. If you will give me your name I will make sure she gets back to you later in the day."

Maggie growled.

"Wait, you can't go in there."

"The hell I can't." Maggie's hand grasped the doorknob.

A seemingly startled Harriet Aristides, in the middle of a phone conference, looked up.

"I want answers and I want them now. What did you do to Lauren, you bitch?"

"James, I need to call you and the team back."

Harry faced Maggie Sullivan and traded ice for ice as their eyes locked in a battle that neither wanted to lose.

Maggie could feel her training ooze out into her mind and demeanor. She had been in dangerous situations enough to know how to deal with predators. Her body straightened and took on the air of superiority. Her voice, although soft and low, had a threatening tone with just a hint of a growl. This bitch is not going to intimidate me. I need answers and I will get them.

"First, if you want answers from me, Ms. Sullivan, you'd better change your attitude."

"Tell me something, Ms. Aristides, do you have a heart?"

"Depends what I need it for."

"All Lauren ever wanted was to find you and know you and how did you respond—with anger and hatred." Her eyes bore into Harriet, wanting to wound her as she had wounded Lauren.

"You blame me? I'm not the one who played the sneak and pretended to be someone she wasn't. Not to mention use someone that I love to get to me. I think anger and hate is tolerable under those circumstances."

Maggie looked at her and smiled. "Oh, really? It seems to me you weren't so forthcoming about your position in this company."

"What the hell are you trying to do? Defend a situation that never should have occurred. If honesty was on the table in the first place, this situation might not have happened."

"Would you have seen Lauren if she told you up front who she was? She didn't use a fake name. What did you want her to do? Shake your hand and say 'oh, by the way we're sisters'." Maggie sucked in a breath. "Nicky knew Lauren wanted to see the head of the company so why didn't she say anything? It seems to me there are more vipers in the nest than just two."

"If you ever, and I mean ever, implicate Nicky in any underhanded dealing, I'll personally kick your butt to the other side of the state," Harry declared.

"That, Ms. Aristides, works both ways. There was nothing, absolutely nothing underhanded about anything Lauren did. She is one of the most honest people I know and you have no right to imply otherwise."

"Really? Guess she's a chip off the old block since she is the daughter of my so-called mother. She's got you fooled, lady." Harry's eyes narrowed. "If I were you, I'd watch out. Next thing you know, she'll run off without a word and leave you all alone. They say things like that run in a family."

The audacity of this woman is unbelievable. "You're amazing," Maggie said. "You don't have a clue about what a family is or who your mother is, for if you did, you never would say such things. Get the facts, Aristides, before you make accusations."

"I think the facts speak for themselves, Ms. Sullivan. My mother left me with my uncle forty years ago, and, to the best of my knowledge, until today, that's been the most contact I've had from her. I could be more brutal in my attitude but in deference to Nicky and her friendship with Lauren, I'll write this particular day off as one where I should have stayed at home in bed."

"You certainly are a piece of work, Aristides. It might serve you to find out all the facts about your mother's contact over the years. I thought you were smarter than that. You haven't even bothered to get all the facts. I feel sorry for you, for you haven't a clue that family is everything."

"You know nothing about me or my family or my lack of it,"

A wry smile crossed Maggie's face. "Oh, I know all about you, and how you think and operate because I was once you."

"Who the hell do you think you are? If you know so much, you won't be surprised at my next comment."

"No I won't, but I can guarantee that you will be sorry for your actions." Maggie turned and started out the door. "I'll save you the trouble of calling security." With that, she was gone. Harry truly hasn't a clue. Wonder if Lauren will ever get an apology...probably not. With swiftly purposeful steps, she walked to the elevator. Her one goal—find Lauren.

∞

Harry gave the closing door a disgusted glance and sat down heavily in her chair. For the first time in her career, she actually wanted her working day to be over early. Damn those women. Did they really think emotional blackmail would work? "It's never worked on me before and it won't now."

Chapter Eleven

When Lauren left the building, she saw a man getting out of a cab and grabbed the open door. "Are you for hire?"

"Sure am little lady, hop on in."

Still distracted and numb, she slid inside and closed the door.

"Where to, little lady?"

"Just drive, I'm not sure yet." She took a quick glance at the building as they drove away and recalled the cold indifference she showed Maggie. She whispered, "I am so sorry." Her mind was whirling with what Harry said and how to fix the mess she created. Where do I go? What can I do? Everything is in shambles. She considered going back to the hotel and waiting for Maggie so they could discuss what to do next. No, I need to work this out on my own. In the back of her mind, she kept hearing Maggie's voice. *There is a long road ahead of us Lauren, but if we go down it together and draw strength from one another, we will make it.* An image of Maggie, who was holding her close and keeping her safe floated into her mind and she knew what she had to do. "Driver, take me to the Regency, downtown."

"Y'all new in town? Thar's lots to see 'round these parts like ..." The driver began his standard Houston chatter with a drawl so thick it was hard, at times, to understand him. That is, if she was paying attention. She wasn't. Her mind was elsewhere as she planned her next move that would convince Harriet Aristides to take a chance on her.

∞

When the taxi pulled to a stop in front of the Regency, Lauren said, "Will you wait for me? I will be about ten minutes."

"Gotta keep the meter runnin,' ya know?"

"I know. Will you wait?"

"Yep. Be right here waitin' for you, little lady."

Lauren tore through the room opening drawers and closets. She rifled through their suitcases and her briefcase until she found what she wanted. She raced back to the waiting cab and jumped in. "Galveston. I need to go to Galveston."

"That's a pretty far piece."

"I know. Can we just go? There's a big tip in it for you." Her heart was racing and she knew the answer to her dilemma was just a cab ride away. "Hurry, please."

Lauren watched the scenery pass by as she wondered if they would ever get to their destination. Cars whizzed past them causing her more agitation and irritation. Her thoughts turned to Maggie, whom she could feel sitting next to her, keeping her safe. She fished in her purse for her cell phone only to find that it wasn't there. "Crap, I gave it to Maggie when I left her to meet Harry." Somehow, she needed to get a message to Maggie and let her know she was ok and that she regretted leaving Maggie the way she did.

As the taxi wound its way through the picturesque town of Galveston, Lauren thought about wandering through the streets with Maggie. That'll have to wait for another time. As the street name of her destination came into view, her heartbeat increased knowing she would have her answers soon.

"Here ya go, little lady. Want me to wait?"

"Yes, please."

"Gonna cost ya more, ya know," the cabbie said.

Lauren said, "I know. I will be back shortly."

For a moment, Lauren stood on the sidewalk outside the magnificent house. She saw the craftsmanship that went into the construction of it and was amazed at the house's condition. The weather conditions on Galveston Island were not friendly to old Victorian buildings. After climbing the stairs, she stood on the wooden porch and looked out over the gulf before ringing the bell. A surge of anticipation went through her body as her heart rate increased when she heard footsteps coming toward the door. The door slowly opened until the person inside was in full view.

"Hello, I'm Lauren Walker."

"Yes, I have been expecting you. Please come in."

She entered, the door closing behind her.

Chapter Twelve

As Sally was returning to her desk after collecting a package for her boss, another secretary said, "I don't know what's going on in Ms. Aristides office, but I heard the shouting out here."

"Oh, no!" Sally hurried back to her desk. Just as she sat down, the door to Harry's office opened. Sally looked at her boss's eyes glaring at her. She swallowed hard and gave a slight smile. "Is everything ok?"

Harry's voice was low ominous. "God, give me strength. If another woman comes anywhere near my office today you have permission to shoot her." Harry turned, and went back in her office slamming the door behind her.

A bewildered and puzzled Sally wondered what had happened in the last half hour. "Okay, I'll shoot 'em boss but what if it's Nicky?" She picked up the mail and began sorting through it when the very woman she was thinking of entered the executive suite. The worried look on Nicky's face had Sally all the more curious about what transpired while she was away from her desk.

"Is there any chance of seeing Harry?" Nicky asked. "I can't say it will be two minutes this time though."

Problems afoot from all corners it would seem. "Well, I'm not sure what's wrong but she told me to shoot any woman who wanted access to her office." Sally studied the young woman's reaction. She saw intense worry. "I think you're the exception to the rule."

A relieved look crossed Nicky's features as she drew in a deep breath. "Thanks."

"Don't thank me until you come out unscathed, Nicky. I've never seen her like this."

Nicky walked to Harry's door and tentatively knocked before she opened it, walked in, and shut the door before Sally heard any retort from Harry.

∞

Irritated by another interruption to her day, Harry glanced up and didn't know whether to grin or grimace. Her heart always did a flip and beat rapidly whenever Nicky entered her personal space, but today was different. She was in a foul mood and didn't want it aimed at her partner. "Nicky."

"You haven't got a loaded gun, have you, Harry?"

"No. No, Nicky, never for you." Harry rushed around the desk and wrapped her arms around her partner.

"Glad to hear it. I waited for your call back but it never came so I thought I'd see if I could help with anything."

Harry bent her head and smelled the fresh herb shampoo that Nicky used and all she wanted was to stay like that. She needed to tell Nicky about the meeting with both Lauren and Maggie, but there wasn't time. In less than half an hour, she had a board meeting and needed her wits about her for that. She wouldn't let anyone, except maybe Nicky, see that she had an Achilles heel. *I didn't when Abby died and I'm certainly not with this new turn of events.* "I love you, Nicky, and thank you for your concern. I promise we'll talk about it tonight. Right now, I need to refocus on business. Okay."

"Harry, whenever is good for you, is good for me." Nicky reached up and ran her fingers through the hair that had strayed over Harry's forehead.

"Thank you. It's just … just …"

Nicky placed a finger on Harry's lips and smiled "It'll wait." She cocked her head to one side before stealing a quick kiss. "Want to buy me a sandwich for lunch?"

Harry let out a sigh for she knew this was Nicky's way of defusing a situation and for that, she was grateful. She shook her head and placed a tender kiss on her lover's lips. Business protocol was something she strictly adhered to unless the situation was severe. She classified the meetings with Lori and Maggie as grave and kissed Nicky again. "I wish I could, Nic, but I really do need to catch up ... it's been a strange day so far."

Nicky smiled. "I'll let you get back to work then."

"Thanks, Nic."

∞

After the confrontation with Harry, Maggie tried to call Lauren only to hear her cell ringing in her pocket. She spent the next two hours calling every Houston cab company trying to find out who picked up Lauren and where she went only to come up empty. Several calls to the hotel room that went unanswered prompted her to go to the Regency and see if Lauren had left her a message.

She slid the keycard into the automated lock and opened the door to their suite. Her eyes narrowed and her brow scrunched in surprise when she saw the disarray. "What happened in here? Lauren?" A sinking feeling gnawed at her gut as her eyes scan the room. Ransacked was the only word she could think of. From her vantage point at the door, she could see papers and other paraphernalia strewn on the floor. Hesitant steps took her farther into the suite and she saw drawers, suitcases, and closets were open with some of the contents scattered on the floor. Her gaze rested on Lauren's opened briefcase with the contents spread across the desk. There was nothing of real value in the room so she dismissed the idea of robbery. With caution, she ventured to the bathroom and found it empty. A quick search of their belongings revealed that nothing was missing. "Where are you, Lauren? What were you looking for?

With that idea in mind, she looked again at their possessions until she came to Lauren's briefcase. She picked up all the papers, neatly arranged them, and then began going through them one by one. What's missing? Where did you go, Lauren? After another investigation of the documents, she realized that the only thing missing was the report her father had compiled about Harriet. "What are you up to, Lauren?" An overwhelming fear gripped her as the full impact of Lauren's disappearance hit her. Maggie wracked her brain trying to remember what was in the report that Lauren could use. She closed her eyes and drifted to the special place where she kept Lauren's spirit and called to her—no reply. There was nothing in the connection she had with Lauren that said she was in trouble but nothing said she was safe either. Where are you?

Maggie knew that chasing all over Houston looking for Lauren was not a smart idea even if that was what she wanted to do. The best alternative was to stay put in their suite and wait for Lauren to call or return to the room.

After she picked up the room, Maggie turned on the television and flicked through channels for the next several hours. Not able to relax, she opened her phone and punched in the number for Harry's home. She hoped Nicky would answer but she was certain that after the shouting match with Harry, the woman would not speak with to her.

∞

Nicky looked with satisfaction at the flowerbed she had weeded. At least one part of the land they had acquired with the house was how she wanted it. She had to admit that the wild look was good in some areas and she'd keep those for the wildlife and birds that had probably made a habitat out of it. Over the next few months she would see exactly what came to reside in the area with them. It was fortunate for her that Harry had no interest in gardening and for that, she was thankful. Harry's choice in house plants was rather bleak. One thing she had found was that Harry loved the fishpond and the bridge that crossed over to the pagoda. With that in mind, she had started in that area first. It would be a wonderful relaxing area for her partner when she came home and needed to relieve the stress. And, that was exactly what she had in mind for this evening. She'd ordered Chinese takeout and since it was a warm night, she figured they could eat outside in the pagoda.

Nicky looked over to the open patio doors of the family room and saw Harry standing tall and magnificent. There were times when she saw Harry and slid into the background so she could watch her for a few precious unguarded seconds. *How did I get so lucky?* She waved and wasn't disappointed as a broad smile crossed her lover's face. She wondered how anyone could put into words what another meant to them. Saying that Harry is everything to me just somehow isn't enough.

Harry strode quickly across the bridge glancing at the fish before she stepped into the pagoda.

Nicky smiled. "You're earlier than I thought?"

Harry replied, "Want me to go away and come back?"

"No, silly." Nicky moved forward and arms wrapped around her in a hug. Then she planted a kiss on Harry's lips that spoke all the words that ever needed to say.

"Want to go to bed early?"

Nicky briefly closed her eyes before she threw Harry a look. "How about you tell me about your day first. After that, I know a wonderful way to relax you."

"Ok."

Nicky listen to Harry tell her version of what happened and felt her emotions go from sadness to anger. She was sad for Harry and Lauren and angry that Maggie tried to force the issue since it was none of her business. When she let her eyes rest on the woman she loved, she realized that it was indeed Maggie's business. That was what partners did. They protect and love each other.

"You're quiet." Harry pulled Nicky closer.

"Sorry. At the moment all I can think is how sad you must feel."

"Sad? Me?" Harry touched her chest. "Why would I be sad?"

Nicky inwardly drew a deep breath before she spoke again. "You have a sister but not in the exact circumstances that would make you happy."

"You can't say that, Nicky. How do I know what she said is true? What proof did she have? None, I tell you, none."

"Do you trust me?"

"You know I do."

"I've known Lauren for years and I would trust her with my life, Harry. She wouldn't lie, I know that."

"How can you know that, Nicky? People change. Look at Eric."

"This is different, Harry. This isn't about money."

"How do you know? You haven't seen her for years. Maybe she thinks I'm a soft touch."

"Soft touch? God, Harry, why would she think that? I've lived with you and believe me, you are not a soft touch ever."

"She wouldn't know that?"

"Exactly, that's why it's not a scam."

"I don't understand?"

They looked at each other—one puzzled the other compassionate until the phone rang.

With her eyes still on Harry, Nicky picked up the phone extension. "Hello."

"Nicky, this is Maggie Sullivan. Please don't hang up."

"What do you want?"

"I don't know who else to call, Nicky. Lauren is missing."

"When did you see her last?"

"Before lunch. She said she needed time to think. Then I came back to our room and found it torn apart."

"Torn apart? Has she been abducted?" Nicky's eyes grew wider.

"Is there a problem, Nicky?" Harry asked, "Who's on the phone?"

Nicky mouthed it was Maggie then nodded that there was a problem.

"No. She was here looking for something then left."

Nicky handed over the phone to Harry who was now standing.

"Have you talked with the front desk?" Harry asked.

"Yes, I have. Do you think I'm a moron? They know nothing. The doorman said he saw her get out of a cab then go inside only to come back out and get in the same cab."

"We will be right there." Harry disconnected and turned weary eyes to Nicky. "I said we'd go over and see what can be done." She took Nicky's hand. "Will you go with me?"

"Try and keep me from it."

"Thank you, Nicky."

"I'll always be there for you." She kissed Harry's cheek. "Let's go, shall we or do you want to change first?"

"There's no time to change. There's no telling what someone will do if emotionally distraught. I would hate to be the one to have caused Lauren to do something stupid."

Nicky smiled and kissed Harry on her lips tenderly. At the heart of the lion there was a pussycat purring. All she needed was care and patience.

As they locked the house, the Chinese meal arrived and Nicky smacked her forehead lightly. "Damn, I forgot about our dinner."

"We'll take it with us. We may be in for a long wait." After paying for the food, Harry dropped the bag on the back seat and climbed in behind the wheel. She put the car into gear and they sped off toward Houston. "Nicky, can I ask you something?"

"Of course. Anything you just name it."

"Are all family situations this fraught?" Her only family life had been with her uncle. He had sent her to all the best boarding schools as soon as she had been old enough. Other than on holidays when she spent time with him and his many woman friends, she never knew what family life was all about. The prospect, however remote, was alien to her. "How does one act with family?"

"Ah, well, this is how families are. You have to take the rough with the smooth." Nicky smiled inwardly.

"So tell me, why have I only ever seen the rough?"

Nicky placed her hand on Harry's knee and squeezed it gently in reassurance. "Maybe when you accept all what a family has to offer, you will reap in the rewards. I promise you that it's worth it."

Chapter Thirteen

The man led Lauren through the foyer into the sitting room. She looked around marveling at the loveliness of the home. Hardwood floors accented with antique oriental rugs set off the well cared for antique furniture. She doubted that the home had changed much from the original structure.

"Won't you have a seat Ms. Walker? Would you like some refreshments?"

"No, thank you. I came in need of answers that only you can provide." She stared at the older man who had, probably at one time, been good looking but now seemed to be suffering from the ravages of an illness. "You said you were expecting me. Why is that?"

The man took a deep breath and looked at her long and hard. "You know, don't you? I've wondered for some time now when your mother or you would show up."

"My mother told me everything. You kept her daughter from her, refusing to let her get to know Harriet in any way. Why, Mr. Aristides? How could you have been so cruel?"

His gait, as he walked toward the window, was slow and uneven. He stared out of a wavy pane of glass before he began to speak in a low voice. "She abandoned her and didn't deserve to have the child. Her attempts to take my precious daughter from me after my brother died were useless. Even when she sent that insipid uncle of hers, I wouldn't relent. Your mother and my brother were never fit to be parents and I needed to protect Harriet from them. Oh, she sent cards, letters, and presents but I just threw them in a box. I saw no need to upset my girl with such foolishness." He turned and smiled. "When she threatened legal action there was nothing she could do, for I had already adopted Harriet. But, I knew one day she would come for her again."

Lauren leveled the man with an angry look. "My mother was sixteen, how did you expect her to act? She certainly wasn't an adult but you were. What exactly did you think you were protecting Harriet from by denying her access to her mother? A mother would have been there to guide her, to love her, and hold her when she was afraid?"

"I gave her all those things. She didn't need your mother." Tears filled his eyes. "Or, so I thought." He suddenly became quiet and returned his attention to the window. "I'm dying, you know."

Lauren nodded. She had suspected as much when she first saw him when he opened the door.

His unsteady gait took him to the mantle where he removed an envelope before turning to Lauren. "This is a letter I was going to leave for Harriet after I died. I think it would be good for her to have it now. I have boxed up all the things her mother sent over the years and will have a courier take them to her immediately. I hope she will find it in her heart to forgive me."

"Why don't you talk to her?"

"I couldn't bear to see the look of hatred in her eyes when she found out what I have done." Tears were freely flowing down his cheeks.

"Have you told her about your illness?"

He shook his head.

"Why not? Don't you think she would want to know?" Lauren reached for his hand and held it.

"I don't want her pity."

"She loves you. She should know. No one deserves to die alone, Mr. Aristides. No one."

"Please, take this letter to your sister for me. From what I understand, her mother needs her now and Harriet should go to her." He handed the letter to Lauren. "Now, if you don't mind, I'm very tired."

He led her to the door and opened it. "Take care, Ms. Walker." He closed the door softly behind her.

∞

Lauren climbed back into the cab and instructed the driver to take her back to the Regency. As she fingered the locket around her neck, her eyes widened. *Maggie. Shit, I never called her. She'll be beside herself with worry.*

"Driver, we need to stop. I need to use a phone."

"K, little lady, thar's one over thar."

Lauren jumped out of the vehicle before it came to a complete stop and walked quickly to the phone booth. "What the hell is the number?" She reached in her pocket taking out the key card and dialed the number. The annoying operator wanted money. *Shit.* Fumbling in her jacket pocket, she found the necessary change and finally heard ringing. "Hello, may I have suite twenty-nine eighty. … Thank you." She waited anxiously, hoping Maggie would be there.

"Maggie? … I know I've worried you. … I am so sorry I didn't call you sooner or leave you a note. … Yes, I'm okay. … I was foolish not to let you know. … Yes, Maggie, I know we need to talk when I get there. … I have wonderful news, Maggie, and I'm on my way there. We need to find Harry and talk with her. I have a letter for her from her uncle. … She's on her way there? … Excellent. Please don't let her leave before I get there in about an hour. … I know you can charm her into waiting. I love you and I am so sorry to have worried you and everyone else. I will be there as soon as possible."

∞

Harry knocked on the door and waited impatiently. She really didn't owe Lauren anything, but for some unknown reason she couldn't keep from worrying about the woman.

The door swung open as Maggie greeted them with a smile. "Hi, glad you came. Come on in."

"What's the situation?" Harry demanded as she walked inside the suite. "I have more important things to do then listen to you rant again."

"Harry, Lori's my friend. If she's in trouble we need to help," Nicky said.

Harry snorted.

"Please stay," Maggie said.

Harry glanced at her watch and turned to attention to Nicky at her side. The look that passed between them made Harry cringe. *Oh no, I've messed up again.* "Sure, we'll stay; what's happening?"

"Thanks."

"How long has she been gone, Maggie?" Nicky asked. "I can't believe she would just take off like that. That isn't something that the Lori I know would do."

"Yeah, it surprised me too." Maggie agreed. "I've been worried sick but she finally called me almost an hour ago."

"Then she's ok?" Nicky asked.

Maggie shrugged. "Apparently so. She has some important news for you, Harry, and asked if you would wait for her."

"I see." Harry clenched jaw. "Let's hope it's more important than the previous information she gave me today."

"Listen, I don't know what your problem is, but I've had enough of you. Do you think this is easy for her or some kind of game?"

Nicky clasped Harry's hand. "I don't think you meant that quite how it came out. Did you, Maggie?"

Harry ignored Nicky's remark. "You tell me. I was never a game player. I wouldn't know."

"Please, sit down. May I get either of you a drink or something to eat?" Maggie turned away from the women then switched back. "Please."

"Thank you, Maggie." Nicky nodded. "We brought the Chinese food that was delivered before we left home. We can share that if you like."

"Thank you for the offer, Nicky. Can it wait until Lauren gets here?"

"Of course. As for something to drink, I'll have water. What about you, Harry?"

"Water is fine for me too." Harry rubbed her temples. "When you called earlier, you said Lauren was missing. Now you tell me she's on her way here. That sounds like a game to me. What exactly am I to think given that set of circumstances?" Harry was upset by the turn of the day's events but she would do her damnedest not to let Maggie know. "Where did she get to or is that a secret as well?"

"Would you believe me if I told you, Harry? The truth is that I don't know what to think either. I came back here expecting to find her. Instead, the room was a mess and she was gone. Then she calls and says she's on her way and has news. It's up to you whether you believe me or not." Maggie blew out a sigh. "I am not interested in our differences, Harry. Lauren is my only focus. Will you please wait for her return?"

Although Harry didn't particularly care for the woman, she knew when someone was telling the truth and Maggie's body language spoke of honesty. It was obvious to Harry that Maggie was still trying to appease her in spite of the obvious dislike she couldn't hide.

"We'll stay. Won't we, Harry?" Nicky laid a hand on Harry's arm. "Let's think of it as one of those fascinating mystery weekends. The only difference is that ours is real."

Harry chuckled inwardly for Nicky was being so Nicky. *She's making light of a potential war zone and somehow everything seems to work out. I'll do anything for her.* "You have my word that we will wait for Lauren's return and I will listen to her news."

"Thank you. I appreciate that very much."

Just then, the door opened and in walked the object of all their discussions and interests.

Maggie went immediately to Lauren and pulled her into a tight embrace. "Are you okay? I've been so worried."

Harry watched the interchange between Lauren and Maggie and instinctively reached for Nicky's hand and held it close to her.

"Good, God, talk of the devil that's bound to return." All eyes traveled to Harry and her attempt at a witty comment.

"Shut up, Harry," Nicky said.

"What? What did I say?"

"I'll explain later." Nicky gave Harry an indulgent nod before looking at her friend. "Lori, are you okay?"

"I am so sorry to have upset everyone, especially you, Maggie." Lauren said.

Maggie drew her close once again.

"Care to share?" Harry was trying not to sound bored with the discussion. She couldn't care less where Lauren was or why she left but it was important to Nicky so she'd do her best to be tolerant.

Lauren stared at Harry intently. "I went to Galveston and visited with your uncle."

Harry merely quirked an eyebrow and gave Lauren a cold calculating look. "And?"

"He gave me this letter for you. Have you seen him lately, Harry?"

"Not lately. He's been abroad and I've been tied up with personal matters." Her glance strayed to Nicky.

"Here is the letter. I think you should visit with him soon, Harry." Lauren placed the letter a few inches from Harry.

Harry took in Lauren's confident stance and applauded the woman's tenacity. *Bit like a terrier after a scrap of food, never giving up.*

"I'll visit with him when and if I see fit. As to the letter, you keep it. He was always susceptible to a pretty face."

"Harry, just take the letter and we'll go," Nicky whispered.

Lauren clenched her jaw. "What is your problem, Harry?"

"Now that you ask, you're my problem. All you've done is deceive me, and now you go behind my back and see my uncle. He's my family. Do you hear me? He's not yours. He has no part in this scheme of yours. I forbid you to ever see him again. Do I make myself clear?"

"As you wish, Harry," Lauren said. "But mark my words; you're making a big mistake." Lauren touched the letter on the coffee table. "Whatever it is you think of me you need to read his letter."

Harry scowled. "Are you stupid? Didn't you understand what I just said?"

"Yes, I did. Thank you for taking the time to come and help Maggie search for me. I'm sorry it has turned out to be a waste of both our time."

"Lady, the only mistake I made was thinking that I was wrong about you." *Who the hell does she think she is? What a prima donna* "Now you have proven that my original judgment wasn't flawed. Perhaps you might take on board the aspect of trust someday and talk to people before you end up weaving elaborate lies that trip you up in the end. If you ever do get to that place in your life, look me up. You might be surprised at the response." Harry walked toward the door and nodded to Maggie before she left.

Harry needed air and took the first available elevator even though she knew she should wait for Nicky. There were times when one had to face the facts and she never really had in regard to her parents. Call it lack of interest, anger, or old childish fears rearing their heads; whatever it was, Lauren made her realize that, come what may, she had to face the demons and decide once and for all what it all meant to her. Perhaps her first port of call should be her uncle. *I'll call him tomorrow and take Nicky with me for a visit.* It would be their first meeting and she wanted the two people she loved most in the world to get to know each other. That and find out the truth.

∞

Maggie watched the exchange with fascination. She had seen the tactic before … the one where you keep baiting until the other explodes giving you a reason to hate. But Lauren hadn't given into that. *That's my girl.* Harry's explosion was way out of proportion to the situation. *I wonder why she's so afraid.*

Nicky hugged Lori. "Hey, it's not all lost. Think about what she's just said. You might be surprised." She hugged her friend closer. "I'll work on Harry. She's a softy, really. You just have to know how to press the right buttons."

Lauren picked up the letter from Harry's uncle and held it out. "Take this. Maybe you can get her to read it. I think it will answer a lot of Harry's questions about her mother and the supposed abandonment."

"I'm going with Nicky down to the lobby. I'll be back soon."

"I will be here when you return," Maggie said.

"Didn't quite work out the way I wanted but as long as there is hope I will keep trying. Thank you for caring." She gave Maggie a big hug before closing the door to follow Nicky to the elevators.

Chapter Fourteen

Maggie turned and went to the phone and pressed the room service button. "Please send my order up now. ... Thank you." She walked into the other room, pulled her suitcase out of the closet, and flung it on the bed. Once opened, she felt around in the side pocket and pulled the object out. She opened the box and recalled the conversation she had with Vicky and Steve several nights before ...

"Vicky, Steve, may I have a few moments with you while Lauren is gone?"

"Certainly, Maggie, have a seat. Do you want a drink?"

"Steven, I don't believe she came to have a drink. Please go on with what you need, Maggie."

"Well, it isn't exactly what I need it is more what you both can give me." She sucked in a deep breath. "As you know, I love your daughter with all my heart."

They both nodded.

"With your permission, I would like to ask her to be my life partner."

Steve was the first to speak. "Maggie, I think it is wonderful you care enough for our feelings to ask our permission." He rose from his seat, went over to Maggie, and gave her a big hug. "Of course, it is all right with us isn't that right, dear?" He looked at his wife. "Is there a problem?"

Victoria's jaw set and Maggie felt her eyes bored into her.

"Why can't you two just be friends?"

"We are friends. Best friends, Vicky."

"Then why have this commitment? Do you have any idea what your lives will be like or how others will stare and whisper about you? Lori isn't strong enough for that."

"She is stronger than you think, Vicky. Of course, we know what will happen. We aren't stupid but we are in love."

"It is unnatural."

"It is natural to us, Vicky. Tell me, when you speak with heterosexual couples do you speculate what goes on in the bedroom?"

"Of course not."

"Then why do you do that with us?"

"Because of the way you have sex."

"Vicky, we don't have sex. We make love. We show each other how much we love each other just as you and Steve do. Besides, it's so much more than that."

"Care to enlighten me, Maggie?"

"When I think of Lauren, my whole body tingles with the sheer delight of knowing that she loves me. She gives me such joy and happiness that there are times I think I will die from the contentment she brings me. She is my best friend and my confidant. I love the person she is. The one you and Steven brought her up to be. She brings a peace that I have never known. My life is complete with her in it and I know she feels the same way. Of course, there will be rough times ahead but they will be insignificant as long as we are together. I want to let her know, as well as our families and friends that I will be in her life always. But, if you say *no*, then I will not mention it again."

"Maggie, I do not doubt your love for my daughter. Do you understand how I feel as a mother, knowing the trials she will have to face being in a homosexual relationship?"

"Yes, I do. So how do you justify your friendship with Ralph and Jeff or is it okay for them but not us? Somehow that doesn't seem fair to me."

"You aren't listening to me at all? I said, as a mother I am worried for my child." Her face softened as she sighed. "I know how much you two love each other, Maggie, and I can't think of anyone who has ever made her as happy as you have. I just worry that's all."

"I know you do, Vicky. Will you trust me to make sure that she is safe and out of harm's way? I think you know, by our actions, that we keep our affections for one another private."

"For more years than I care to remember, Lori and I have been at odds and it was heartache for both of us. Along you came and in a matter of weeks, my daughter and I were talking once again. That was something I never could seem to accomplish. The bottom line Maggie, I'm jealous of you." A single tear trickled down her cheek.

In a flash, Maggie was kneeling in front of Vicky, taking her hand as she smiled. "Vicky, Lauren was on her way back to you long before I came into the picture. Why do you think she came when she did? It was to have you back in her life again. Don't you how much she loves you? It was never my intention to take her away from you, family is far too important to us both for that. Why do you think we chose Warwick to make our home?"

A long sigh, of what seemed to Maggie like relief, came from Vicky.

Vicky's face creased into a smile. "Welcome to the family, Maggie."

A knock at the door brought her out of her reverie. She opened the door and allowed the waiter to enter, place the tray on the coffee table, signed the receipt, and tipped him before he left.

Now, to wait for Lauren to return. I'm so nervous. What if she says no? The thought had never occurred to her but now that it had, she began thinking of all sorts of scenarios of how she would plead with her to say *yes.*

The sound of the door opening sent a tingle down Maggie's spine. Lauren always had that effect on her when she was near. In all honesty, she knew that the very thought of her did it every time.

"Hey, what is this?" Lauren smiled broadly looking at the tray with champagne, strawberries, and roses. "Is it a special occasion that no one told me about?" She laughed as she went over to Maggie and engulfed her in her arms.

"It could be. Depends on you, really." Her arms wrapped around Lauren, pulling her close. "Do you know how much I love you?" Her voice was strong and resolute but there was a hint of concern that she could not mask.

Lauren frowned. "Maggie, is this how you dump someone? With champagne and strawberries?"

Maggie let out a hearty laugh as she pulled Lauren closer. A loving smile crossed her face as she bent to kiss trembling lips. "I could never leave you. You are my life and my love." She took the smaller hand, led her to the couch, and both sat down.

"Lauren, in my life I have never known the happiness you have given me. When we are together, I feel joy and peace that takes over my entire being and when we are apart, it is your love that sustains me." With a firm hold of Lauren's hand, Maggie placed a ring on her finger. "Lauren Walker, will you do me the honor of being my life partner?"

Tears cascaded down her cheeks as Lauren grinned. "I will do you one better. I will be your partner for all eternity and beyond. I think that from the moment that I saw you crawl out of the river, I have loved you. You held the key that unlocked my heart." A brilliant smile crossed her face. "Yes, I will be your partner for now and forever."

Tears began falling down Maggie's cheeks. "You've made me the happiest woman in the world." She gently kissed Lauren's lips. "I had this ring made especially for you."

"It's beautiful, Maggie."

"The diamond on either side represent our souls, the heart shaped diamonds next to them our hearts and the large heart diamond in the middle are our hearts and souls as one." Maggie reached for the tray on the coffee table and placed a strawberry in a glass then poured in some champagne and offered the glass to Lauren. "For you, my love."

Lauren sipped the champagne then offered Maggie the glass. "For you, my love."

Maggie took the strawberry out of the glass and traced Lauren's lips with it. Lauren captured the fruit between her lips and Maggie's lips surrounded the other half as their lips met. Maggie was the first to pull back as she sensuously licked her lips before chewing and swallowing the strawberry.

Soon Maggie succumbed to passion as lips feverishly sought out hers and fingers tore at buttons and hooks. She whispered declarations of love as sensual moans filled the air. Her body slid against Lauren's and they merged into one.

Maggie was so engrossed in her lover that she did not hear the phone's incessant ringing. When the phone rang for the third time, Maggie picked up the receiver. "Hello. It's for you." Maggie handed the phone to Lauren.

"Yes? .. Oh, hi, Harry. ... "Yeah, see you then. Bye."

Lauren let out a satisfied sigh. "Harry will pick us up at nine. Her company's jet will take us to Warwick."

"What made her change her mind?"

"My guess is she read her uncle's letter." Lauren paused then looked at Maggie. "He's dying and doesn't want her to know."

"Is that what was in the letter?"

"I don't know."

"Then you must tell her before we take off tomorrow. How long do you think he has?"

"I don't think he was on death's doorstep but his skin was sallow and he looked frail." Lauren shook her head. "I can't break his trust by telling Harry, Maggie. He said he wrote the letter for Harry to see after he died. I have no other recourse but to honor his request." Lauren's eyes widened. "She's actually going with us to Warwick. That is so awesome. We need to pack and I need to call my folks. Mom is going to be so pleased."

Maggie laughed.

"What?"

Maggie spread her arms. "Here I am, naked and ready, and Harry calls. She has to be family for who else would have such lousy timing."

Lauren laughed. "Another sign that this is all going to work out perfectly."

Chapter Fifteen

"You know you could have been kinder." Nicky scolded when they returned home.

"I could? Please tell me how could I be *kinder* when she wants me to go see someone who means less to me than a stranger I give the odd few coins to in the street?"

"You don't do that, Harry. You tell them to get a job."

"Exactly my point."

Exasperation and disbelief filled Nicky's senses as she heard the cold precise words from Harry. *She doesn't mean it. How can she? We're talking about her mother and not some panhandler.* "Harry?"

"Yes."

"Anyone ever tell you that you are a stubborn pig headed mule?"

Harriet leveled a serious glance at her. "No."

"Well, take it from someone who knows you reasonably well, you are."

"Shit, Nicky. You don't know what you're talking about and you don't mean it."

"Really? Well I suggest you provide evidence to make me change my mind."

"Why should I?"

Nicky knew she was running a fine line with Harry. They had never really argued and she didn't know why she was challenging her now. It was true that Harry's mother had abandoned her but something about the whole situation that didn't ring true to her.

Her mind refused to let that concern rest. "No reason really. Do you know why after all these years you refuse to accept that someone could have made a mistake? If it were me, I'd like to see the person who decided I wasn't worth the bother. I'd want answers to why she abandoned me and why the sudden interest after forty years. I'd want her to know how much it hurt me."

Harry shook her head. "I'm confused. Exactly what are you trying to tell me?"

Nicky's heart raced at the words. *She knows so much but is very naïve when it comes to the delicate and intrinsic workings of human emotions.* Harry was a baby in the emotions department and went at problems as if she were dealing with board members. "I'm trying to say …"

The doorbell sounded and both looked toward the hall.

Harry moved toward the door. "Who could it be at this hour?"

Ten minutes later, Nicky looked at several boxes that a courier had dropped off. She looked at Harry who had a puzzled gaze. "You know, Harry, you could always open one."

"Yes, I know that." Her hands stripped one of the boxes of its strapping.

Nicky watched Harry who began unwrapping the smallest package in slow motion. Her thoughts returned to their conversation and her challenge. Harry had at least been civil with Lauren and didn't completely rule out seeing her mother. In fact, until she mentioned that Harry should see her mother, she could almost say that Harry was getting to know Lauren and liked what she saw. She sensed her partner's distress as silence filled the room.

Harry was standing completely still with a sheaf of letters, which were tied together with a piece of innocuous twine in her hand.

Nicky's eyes moved toward the bundle that Harry clenched tightly in her fist. "Anything interesting?" The silence stretched as Nicky noted that Harry's eyes blinked several times as if she were trying to understand the significance of what she held in her hand. That sight alone confused Nicky, for Harry could always to assimilate information quickly.

"Are you okay?"

Harry blinked several times more before staring in Nicky's direction. "I'm not sure."

Nicky gently reached for the letters that motionless fingers held and extracted them. She glanced at first the recipient and then the sender on the back of the envelope.

"To: Ms Harriet Aristides, from Ms Victoria Maxwell"

"Who's Victoria Maxwell?"

Harry replied, "My mother."

"I thought your mother was Victoria Walker?" For the first time in what seemed liked hours, Harry smiled and Nicky knew that things were going to be okay. Harry placed her arm around her and hugged her tenderly.

"She is. That was her maiden name. The date on that letter you have in your hand is thirty-three years ago, I was nine at the time."

Nicky's eyes went as wide as it clicked into place exactly what it meant. Victoria Walker had never totally abandoned her daughter. "Harry, to me, this doesn't look like someone who didn't want to know you. Come on; let's open up more of the packages."

Harry reluctantly complied and let Nicky do most of the unwrapping.

Half an hour later, Nicky looked at the numerous letters that surrounded them. Presents of every description joined the letters. Dolls, books, clothes, pens, paint, and just about anything, a child could want rested on the floor. All the packages were still in their original wrappings, just as they were when delivered to her uncle's address.

"Shall we put the things in date order, especially the letters, and read them?" Nicky was excited and her enthusiasm took over as she started the process before seeing the uncertainty in Harry's eyes. When she received no answer, she looked up and caught the disbelief and something she couldn't put a finger on, in the depths of Harry's eyes. *Is that torment?*

"I … I think I'll get us a drink. You do what you think is best."

Harry strode off toward the liqueur cabinet, leaving Nicky somewhat unsure as to how to proceed.

∞

A couple of minutes later, Harry stood with a drink in one hand staring out of the patio windows onto the serenity of the garden. An entire lifetime of preconceptions she had about her mother, abandoning her and not giving a damn didn't hold water anymore. *Can it be all a lie? Why now? Why has my uncle kept this information from me? It doesn't make any sense.*

Harry felt the tension of the situation building and she didn't know what to do. As that thought crossed her mind, arms engulfed her in a warm, loving hug. Nicky's arms settled around her like a blanket. She felt all the tension ease as she gazed into the face of the woman who had that effect on her life and on every single level there was.

"I love you, Harry."

"I know you do and I love you so very much. Thank you."

Nicky's eyebrows quirked. "For what?"

"For being you, for simply being you. Please never change."

"No chance of that, no chance at all. Shall we put all that stuff away? You can make me a drink and we'll relax. What do you say to that idea?"

Harry kissed the tempting lips and her reward was a rather delicious assault that took her breath away. Just as every kiss she shared with Nicky always did. Once they stopped kissing, Harry smiled. "Tell you what. You get some of those letters, I'll make a phone call, and we'll have that drink."

"Sure thing."

Harry picked up the phone, punched in numbers, and waited until someone finally answered.

"I'd like to speak to Lauren. … Lauren, I've decided to visit Victoria. I'll pick you up at nine in the morning, my company's jet will take us to Warwick. See you tomorrow, bye."

She replaced the receiver on the cradle, decanted a decent bottle of white wine, and retrieved two glasses. As she walked back into the room, she saw Nicky engrossed in the letters and presents that were stacked around her. "You look like you're in Santa's grotto."

With a bright smile on her face, Nicky's shook her head and motioned for Harry to sit on the floor next to her.

"I think this was the first one, it's dated the year you were five, I think. Shall we start with this?"

"Okay, is there a letter from my uncle in all this?"

"Yes. Here it is. Want to read this first?"

"You choose." Harry poured them both a glass of wine and settled down close to Nicky who appeared to be contemplating what to read first.

"I guess we should or you should read what your uncle has to say first."

"If these were yours, what would you do?"

Nicky said, "One of Victoria's."

"Then one of Victoria's, it will be. Will you read it to me, please?"

"I'd be honored; thank you."

When Harry inclined her head slightly, Nicky settled onto her chest and her in a warm loving embrace. She then began …

My Darling Daughter Harriet,

This is my first letter to you. You might think it strange that I'm writing and not seeing you. Perhaps when you are a little older we will do that too.

I've sent along a special friend with this letter. I hope you can love him and when you look at him think of me from time to time. I even gave him a name, Clarence. You will no doubt change it but I'll always think of him as Clarence the Lion. Perhaps you might write and tell me what you called him and then I shall know for the future.

I will make this short, as young ladies usually do not want to spend time going over long correspondence. At least, I didn't at your age. I'm in college right now. It is my first semester toward my Law Degree. Who knows, your mother may be a big shot lawyer one day.

I love you, Harriet, even though circumstances are forcing us apart at the moment. Trust that I'm coming to get you as soon as I can keep us both.

All my love,
Your Mother

Nicky folded the letter and placed it back in the envelope. "There it is." Nicky looked at Harry. "What?"

"Clarence." Harry pointed to a golden soft toy lion that was magnificent.

"Would you have called it anything else?" Nicky asked.

Harry shook her head. "No, Clarence is about right."

"I love you, Harry, so much it hurts."

Both women hugged each other tightly for a few minutes. Harry reluctantly released Nicky as she reached over to select her uncle's letter.

"Do you want to read it alone?"

"No. No, you are more a part of me than any other living being ever could be. I want you to share every part of my life."

"Thank you. You don't know what that means to me."

"I do, Nicky, if it means even half to you what it means to me."

Harry flicked the letter open and began to read her uncle's letter aloud …

Dear Harriet,
This may come as a complete surprise and then again, it may not. I don't regret the actions I took all those years ago and given the time over again, I would do exactly the same thing.

I was a bachelor with a career and suddenly my brother deposited a child on my doorstep. Perhaps that is rather melodramatic of me. When my brother and his child bride went off on their journeys, they left you with me to care for. Frankly, your father didn't want the responsibility of a child and your mother went along with his wishes. Therefore, you came into my life.

When Vicky's letters and presents started to arrive, I didn't know what to do, and I hid them thinking that I would give them to you at a later date. Somehow, it never happened. I guess you will rightly be upset with me and I am sorry for that for I never wanted to hurt you intentionally.

Love sometimes makes you do strange things and in all my life, this is the strangest I've ever undertaken. I continually lied to the only person that I love and have loved since fate placed you in my arms as a six-week-old baby.

All I ask is for you to try to forgive my deception and know I would never harm you. Harriet, you are to all intents and purposes, my daughter and always will be.

Warmest Regards,
Uncle Harry

Harry held in Nicky's arms and wondered why she didn't cry for all the wasted years she never knew her mother. Or, for the hurt that her uncle felt when he thought of Victoria taking his precious surrogate daughter from him. It was a tragic a situation for all of them. They all lost on love in their lives. *Perhaps now is a good time to resolve the hurt, jealousy, and guilt garnered over the years.*

"Don't you think we need to speak to Lauren?" Nicky asked.

"I've already taken care of that."

"What about your uncle?"

A shudder ran through Harry. "I don't know."

"I'll be right there beside you, Harry. I'll hold your hand or whatever else you need."

"You will?"

"Oh, yeah. Wherever you go, I'm right there beside you to the end. Preferably a happy end."

"He'll like you."

Nicky beamed. "I like him already."

Harry grinned at the remark. No matter what, her Uncle was the only person who had given her love for those years. Albeit it was in small doses but it was love nonetheless and she loved him as she would a father. *Perhaps it is time I tell him.*

"After we go to Warwick, it's on to see my uncle. Is that okay with you?"

"You're the boss." Nicky hugged Harry close. "Do you think you should give him a call now? He probably is frantic about your reaction. I know I would be."

"You're right. I will give him a call in the morning before we go and let him know we will be visiting after we get back from Warwick."

As Nicky nestled closer, Harry found herself enveloped in a hold that held a promise for today and the future. Together they would make it, no matter what hurdles they saw before them.

Chapter Sixteen

Lauren and Maggie expressed their love late into the morning hours; feeling, tasting, speaking, seeing, and smelling love. The last barriers were gone, as they became one in mind, body, and spirit. When sleep finally took them, they were snuggled together in such a way that you could not tell where one began and the other started. It was as it should be, as it had been throughout the ages—two souls as one, once again.

Lauren was the first to open her eyes. Feeling Maggie close to her brought a smile of satisfaction across her face as she recalled what she could only describe as a spiritual experience. Lauren closed her eyes; she allowed her body to drift into a sexual haze, slowly molding her body around Maggie's warm body. Once again, she opened her eyes and gazed around the room where they committed completely to one another. It was the typical hotel bedroom, perhaps a bit more pretentious than most, holding the customary amenities and furniture. Then she saw it, and terror filled her entire body.

"Shit! Maggie, wake up, wake up now."

"Uh? What's the matter, Lauren?" Maggie squinted one eye open looking closely at Lauren. "Is this how you're going to wake me up from now on? I can tell you it doesn't put me I …"

"Hush. They'll be here in twenty minutes."

"What the hell are you talking about?"

"Harry."

"Oh, shit. Okay, you go jump in the shower and I'll start getting things packed. Are we meeting them here or downstairs? Oh, it doesn't matter. Leave it up to me. I'll take care of everything," Maggie said

Lauren gave Maggie one more kiss before she headed for the bathroom. "Love you."

∞

Maggie watched Lauren as she walked away and her heart filled with happiness. "No time for those thoughts, girl." She laughed and picked up the phone.

After arranging for the bill, Maggie called room service for coffee, tea, juice along with a bread and fruit basket. She dialed another number and waited for an answer.

"Good morning, Harry, this is Maggie. ... Listen, we are running a little late ... Yes, I know the importance of being on time, Harry. It's just ... I know you don't appreciate being kept waiting. ... Will you let me get a word in edgewise, Harry ... I understand that, Harry. But you know, sometimes life just doesn't want to keep to a schedule. ... It's not an excuse I was merely stating a fact. ... Not that I owe you anything, but last night I asked Lauren to be my life partner and she accepted. We celebrated late into the morning. ... Don't worry, Harry, we won't keep you that long. I've ordered a light breakfast that should be here when you arrive. I need to get ready now. Bye."

Maggie hung up the phone. "*Congratulations are in order then.* I can't believe her condescending tone when she said that. Up yours, lady. I can't believe that woman and Lauren are related." She scanned the room and saw the unfinished bowl of strawberries and her heart stood still as a sense of total peace came over her. She placed her hand over her heart—it was still beating.

"Are you okay?"

Maggie smiled. "I'm wonderful. Come over here please?"

Maggie took Lauren's hand and placed it over her quietly beating heart. "It beats for you and only you."

Lauren took Maggie's larger hand and placed it over her heart. "As mine does only for you."

Their bags were packed and ready by the door when Harry and Nicky arrived. Not a small feat by any standards but they did work well together. For Maggie there was the added irritant of Harriet Aristides and her superior attitude that made her work double time to be ready when they arrived.

Lauren opened the door with the first knock. "Hi, come on in."

As the two women entered the room, Maggie eyed the tall one with contempt. "We're ready to go when you are, Harry." She glanced at her watch. "And right on time. We've ordered a light meal if you would like or we can go right now. It's your choice."

Harry glared. "Thank you, it looks good."

"Please, sit down." Lauren smiled. "We have coffee or tea and I see we have juice also. Maggie, you think of everything."

All the anger left Maggie with that one smile. "Why don't I go downstairs, settle the bill, and arrange for someone to get our bags." She kissed Lauren gently on the cheek. "Back in a flash."

"Excuse me for a minute." Lauren followed Maggie to the door. "Is something going on I should know about?"

"Nothing at all love, just a slight case of not letting others get under my skin. It will be fine, I promise."

∞

Once the door closed, Lauren turned to her guests only to hear her cell phone ring.

"Hello. … Just a moment." Lauren looked at Harriet and Nicky. "I'll take this in the other room, be right back." Lauren disappeared into the bedroom, "Daddy, it is so good to hear your voice. I have so much to tell you. We will be on our way home shortly and Harry will be with us. … What is wrong? Is it Mom? … "What sort of infection? Does she have the same doctors? Do you want me to call them? … I have the utmost confidence in Doctor Green. … Tell her we will be there this afternoon by one, two at the latest. … Bye, Daddy."

Laruen re-entered the room. "I'm sorry. I had to take that call. I'm glad to see that you helped yourselves." She poured herself some coffee, and sat down next to Nicky.

"Are you okay?" Nicky asked.

"Yes. I'm just a bit overwhelmed with all that is happening at once." She held out her left hand. "Look what Maggie gave me last night."

"Oh, Lori, that is beautiful."

"Yes it is. She asked me to be her life partner."

Nicky gave her friend a warm embrace. "I'm so happy for you."

"Congratulations," Harry mumbled.

Chapter Seventeen

The limo driver opened the door for the women and they disembarked from the vehicle.

Maggie, who was the first to enter the airport, noticed several of her father's men positioned around the area. *Still watching over us I see.* She had called her father earlier to tell him of her plans.

Harry walked quickly past everyone. "Follow me. We are going to the VIP Lounge."

Maggie recognized the man soon as she saw him. She held her breath as she passed by him in hopes that he wouldn't recognize her. With her new face, hair, and eye color she knew there couldn't be a problem. This was the first time that she had seen anyone she recognized from the old days. He was clearly involved with his newspaper as she passed by unnoticed and she let out a sigh of relief.

"I'd know that walk anywhere. CJ wait up."

Shit. Maggie and the other women kept walking showing no signs of recognition.

The man persisted. "CJ, don't you recognize me?" The man grabbed Maggie's arm and spun her around.

Maggie had two choices—stand and fight or run. She had been in the business long enough to know it was always best to confuse your opponent. After all, this was an airport filled with the police.

Maggie let out a wail. "Someone help me. This man is trying to attack me!"

Harry, Nicky, and Lauren all turned around.

Lauren knitted her eyebrows.

"No, no I am not. CJ, it's me, Tommy. Please stop screaming."

Police officers came rapidly to the terrified woman's aid and pulled the man away from her.

"Oh, thank you, Officers. I think he wanted to steal my bag." Maggie shrunk away from the man. "Please take him away."

"No I wasn't. I'm sorry, lady. I thought you were someone I knew. I was mistaken. Sorry."

About that time Lauren appeared by Maggie's side. "Maggie, are you all right? Did this man frighten you? Officers, she is very high strung and after nine eleven she's terrified of airports."

Maggie was trembling. "No, Lauren, you're wrong. He tried to attack me. He probably wanted me to carry something for him on the plane."

"Don't worry, ma'am, we will question him. He won't bother you anymore."

Lauren whispered, "He recognized you?"

Maggie took Lauren's arm and headed them back to their companions. "Yes."

Harry looked at Maggie. "What was that all about?"

"That weirdo was trying to accost me. The police have taken care of him." The intensity with which Harry was scrutinizing her, unnerved Maggie but she wasn't about to let it show.

"I see. Why don't you all sit here and I will check on our plane. Be right back."

"Harry, why don't I walk with you?" Nicky said.

∞

"Okay, Maggie, give. What was that all about?"

At the same moment, one of the men working for Maggie's father approached them and signaled for Maggie to come with him.

"I will be with you in a few minutes, Rick. Lauren, the man who came up to me works for the man that thinks I am dead. Can you believe it? I went through all that surgery and he recognized me by my walk. Isn't that the most ironic thing you've ever heard?"

"What will happen now?"

"Not sure. I will know more once I talk with Rick." Maggie held the smaller hand trying to console Lauren but knew she was failing miserably.

"Then go talk to him, I'll wait here."

"Be right back, promise." Maggie rose from the seat and quickly walked over to the waiting man. They stood talking for several minutes before she returned to Lauren.

She sat down and looked deep into Lauren's eyes. Maggie wanted to take Lauren away but she knew she couldn't. If they didn't work quickly, they would all be in danger. "I can't go to Warwick with you. The police are holding the man, but it won't be for long. Right now, we need to work fast to erase any evidence of my being here."

Lauren shook her head.

"We don't have any other choice. These men are killers and now you, Harry, and Nicky could be in danger if I don't work fast to distance myself from all of you. I won't allow that, Lauren."

Tears were beginning to form in Lauren's eyes. "How long? No wait. I can go with you and help you."

Maggie gently caressed Lauren's face. "I won't be long. You can't go with me, Lauren. I can't put you in that sort of danger. If anything ever happened to you I would not survive." A lone tear cascaded down her cheek. "I love you. You're everything to me, Lauren. You *are* my everything."

Maggie hugged her tight. "I will be right there with you wherever you are, Maggie. Hurry home to me. We have a ceremony to plan."

Maggie gently kissed the tear stained cheek. "You have my cell number. You can reach me anytime you need to." Then, gazing into the eyes she loved, Maggie smiled. "I'll be back in a flash. Count on it."

"Come back safe," Lauren said.

∞

Harry saw Lauren sitting alone. Maggie was nowhere in sight. *Damn her, the plane is ready and she is off ... doesn't she understand plans and schedules at all.* "We're all ready to board, Lori. Where's Maggie? I hope she won't be too long."

"She won't be going with us."

Harry took a seat next to Lauren. "What's the matter, Lauren?" *If she's dumped her here in this airport, I will hunt her down and make sure she is sorry.* "Has something happened between you and Maggie? Has she hurt you?" Concern for someone else was not something that came easily to Harry but she could feel a bond forming with the woman.

"Oh, no. Nothing like that at all, Harry."

"I know tears when I see them, Lori."

Lauren smiled. "I always cry when we are separated, Harry. I love her that much."

"Then where is she?" *Something is going on. I know it.*

"The police need her to stay here while they interrogate the man that accosted her. She already has tickets for a later fight and will join us tomorrow. It's not a problem. Really."

"I see. Well then, shall we be on our way. Nicky has already boarded." *There is more to this and I will get to the bottom of it.* She hoped that Lauren would confide in Nicky as to what the real story was.

∞

Harry and Lauren boarded the aircraft as the doors shut behind them. Nicky looked at them puzzled. "Didn't you forget someone? Where's Maggie?" Seeing the tear streaks down Lori's cheeks, she looked immediately at Harry. "There hasn't been a problem between you and Maggie already, has there?"

Harry's eyes opened wide. "Nic, why would you say that?"

"No, no, Nicky, Harry has nothing to do with it. The police needed Maggie for questioning about the man who accosted her. She didn't want to delay our trip so she taking a later flight and will be with us later today or tomorrow. There isn't a problem."

With a face reddened by embarrassment, Nicky let her eyes settled on her partner. "Harry, I'm sorry. You and Maggie have been so contentious that I jumped to the wrong conclusion." She shrugged. "Can you forgive an idiot like me?"

Harry gazed at Nicky. "Of course." She sat down next to Nicky, took her hand, and kissed it. "I do love you with all my heart, Nicky."

After the plane took off, Nicky watched Lauren walk over to the table where Harry was going over documents. "May I have a moment of your time?"

Harry looked up. "Of course. What can I do for you?"

"It is more what I can tell you than anything else."

"Really, is there something more you forgot to tell me?"

"Not really. There hasn't been any time to tell you since I found out."

"Exactly what is it that you found out, Lauren?"

"Is there a problem here?" Nicky joined the women.

"Your friend here has some news for me that she didn't feel fit to tell us on the ground."

"No, it isn't that way at all, Harry. Will you just give me a chance to speak before you jump to conclusions?" Lauren bit down hard on her lip.

"By all means, little sister, do tell."

"When you arrived this morning I received a phone call from my father." Lauren explained. "They have taken my mother—our mother—to the hospital so we will have to visit her there. Is that okay with you, Harry?"

"I see. That won't be a problem. Now, if you don't mind, I have some work to do." Harry turned her head and began reading the reports.

Nicky began to open her mouth but then thought better of it and walked back to her seat with Lauren.

Chapter Eighteen

"Harry, are you okay?" Lauren hadn't seen her newly discovered sister so somber and withdrawn. She was normally larger than life and very vibrant, yet now, as they were about to enter their mother's hospital room, she was like a wax statue.

"Perfect."

"I'll fetch coffee, be back in a few minutes," Nicky said.

Harry merely nodded numbly as she and Lauren entered the room. Lauren gazed at her mother and saw a sallow face with a frail appearance lying in the bed. She sucked in a deep breath.

"Harriet, hi, I'm Steve Walker, Victoria's husband and Lauren's father. Welcome."

Harry inclined her head slightly in acknowledgement. "Hi."

Steve glanced at his daughter who nodded that it was ok for him to leave. "Well, I guess I'll leave you ladies alone. Have a nice chat." Steve turned to his wife and winked. His reward was a loving smile.

"Thank you, darling. I'll see you shortly."

"Count on it." Steve bent down to kiss his wife on the cheek. "You'll see that everything will work out."

Lauren moved closer to her father before hugging and kissing him.

Once the door closed behind Steven, Victoria looked at her long lost daughter. "Harriet, it is so good to see you. I apologize it has to be in the hospital rather than in our home."

"Victoria."

It was impossible for Lauren not to feel the undercurrents of anger in her sister. Her mother, although gravely ill, was at least trying. Harry was not. "Is there any merit in me being the go between?"

Harry glowered at Lauren.

She got the message. "Okay, how about I go help dad and Nicky with refreshments." It wasn't a question. Without looking back at the other two, she quickly exited the room.

"I think they want us to be alone. Is that okay with you, Harriet?"

"I guess." Harry glanced around the room taking in every angle and piece of equipment she could. She refused to look at the woman lying in the bed.

"You guess. Can't you be a bit more positive?"

Harry flushed at the comment. That wasn't part of the deal. She was the one supposed to be in charge of the conversation not her mother. She needed to be the one asking questions and getting answers. "Why?"

Victoria gulped in a deep breath then exhaled slowly. "I won't insult your intelligence by asking what you mean. I was sixteen years old and helplessly in love with your father. We didn't have a home base, we thought it best…"

"*We* as in my father and you decided that it was for the best? You both made the decision. Were you married when I was born?" Harry, not knowing why she asked such a question, could only stare at the woman who was her mother.

"Yes, we got married three months before you were born. We were young and in love and Rob wanted to travel the world. I worshipped him and would have followed him anywhere and did." Victoria lifted one shoulder.

"Oh, please, save me from the lovey dovey trite comments. At the end of the day, you left me with Uncle Harry and never came back."

"We never intended it to be long term."

"Long term?" Harry didn't try to hide her anger. "For Christ sake. Long term? I'm forty one almost forty two, you call that short term?"

"I call it a mistake. I've paid for it every single moment since I left you with Harry." Victoria desperately tried to have eye contact with Harry but she turned her head away. "I wrote you."

Harry felt split between the anger she wanted to expend and the reality that the woman, who had abandoned her, had tried to keep contact. She couldn't make any major decision about her biological mother until she had a chance to speak with her uncle.

"You do know don't you that what you did sucks big time. I'm going to see my uncle and he might help me piece together this jigsaw puzzle."

"I doubt it," Victoria said. "Your uncle was ... how should I put it ... extremely possessive of you. I don't blame him for you are a very beautiful and accomplished woman. He should be very proud of the terrific job he did raising you on his own."

"I'm sure he's suitably happy with how I turned out." Harry turned away fully this time to look out of the window.

∞

As Victoria gazed at her daughter, she saw Rob in the way she stood. It was so like him to weigh the conversation intelligently so he'd know how to react. *Just as Harry is doing now. Or am I dreaming that I can see so much of my first love in our child.* Victoria had looked into the depth of her daughter's eyes earlier and knew how expressive they were. *They talk to my very soul just as Rob's did.* She felt certain Rob would have been proud of his offspring, although she doubted he would have had much to do with his child. Family life was not on his agenda and with his free spirit, had he lived, he would not have stayed around to see his daughter grow up. *Would I?* Victoria never asked that question herself before.

Vicky watched as Harry moved away from the window and paced the floor incessantly. *Maybe she's as nervous about this initial meeting as I am.* She could only imagine what those that consider her a solid immovable judge would think if they knew how frightened she was of meeting her daughter after so many years. The overwhelming sadness she always felt when she thought of the daughter she left with Rob's brother made her stomach churn. "You're not a conversationalist are you?"

"It depends on who I'm talking to and the content of the conversation," Harry declared.

"Are you happy, Harriet? That is the only thing that matters to me. If you accept me or not isn't as important to me as knowing if you are happy."

"I'm successful. I do what I want and don't have to listen to anyone about my life, so yeah, I'm happy."

Vicky wasn't content with the answer. "Are you in a relationship that makes you happy? Do you have a husband, a lover, or a good friend?"

Harry turned and stared at Victoria in surprise. "I'm a loner and happy to be so. People come and go and it doesn't matter to me." The words were hardly out of her mouth when the door opened.

Victoria recognized the woman in the doorway but couldn't place who she was. The girl's face looked distraught as she stood there holding a cup of what looked like coffee.

"Here's your coffee," she said.

Before Harry could reply, the woman had put the cup down and left the room.

Victoria wasn't sure what to make of the incident. Her new found daughter became even more morose than she had been.

∞

Nicky didn't know what to do as she closed the door of the hospital room. Did she really hear Harry say she was a loner and needed no one? *It isn't true. I know it. Or do I?* She had felt her heart heave a sigh of relief when she heard the tone in Harry's voice. She was speaking to her mother in a voice that wasn't condescending or angry but one that was calm and controlled, bordering on boredom. It wasn't until the words pierced her consciousness that she felt a heavy weight fall on her shoulders and ring out all around her. The fact that Harry didn't attempt to display any remorse over her comment that she knew Nicky heard wounded her deeply. The entire situation was becoming more and more complicated with every passing hour. She sucked in a calming breath. *What else can possibly crawl out of the woodwork?*

On their way to get coffee, she and Lauren spoke about the joining ceremony Lauren and Maggie were going to have as soon as Victoria recovered enough to attend. It had made Nicky feel good for them and wondered if she and Harry might have a joining ceremony at some stage. *Perhaps I should propose to Harry and find out.* It was with those thoughts that she took the coffee to Harry and heard the words that broke her heart.

∞

Harry placed a hand over her mouth. "Damn it." *So much for trying to be spiteful. I should have just told Victoria about Nicky and be done with it.* She had been in enough meetings in her life to know that stupid one up-man ships always ended in a mess. She needed to find Nicky and explain.

Harry, completely ignoring Victoria, started for the door.

"Please drink your coffee and come sit by me. I'd like to tell you about your father,"

Harry stopped. Ever since she was a child and understood about parents, she had always wanted to know about her father. Her uncle had called him a gypsy or worse. But she had imagined something completely different. Her father had never let her down for he died when she was three years old. She clung to the notion that if he lived he would have come back for her to be a family, a proper family.

"I need to see my friend." Her hand reached toward the door.

"I see. Well, I was getting tired anyway. Will you be here tomorrow?"

Harry briefly closed her eyes and turned back. This might be her only chance to find out about her father. *Who better to explain things than this woman?*

Nicky will understand when I explain it to her later on. I know it. "No, I'm going to see Harry tomorrow. Why don't you tell me about my father now?"

Victoria smiled. "I'd like that. Where do you want me to start?"

Once she moved closer to the bed, Harry settled in a chair to the left of her mother and pursed her lips as she pondered an answer. "When you first met him, what was he like?"

For the first time since she heard that Harriet was visiting her, Victoria felt at ease. "I met him when I was fifteen years old. He was the most handsome boy; rugged, dark hair and with the most sensual blue eyes I've ever seen. He was also three years older than I was and worked on the midway at the fair. I knew he was wild." She smiled. "He was so charming and all the girls were crazy over him. When he chose me, I fell instantly and madly in love."

∞

Nicky sucked in a deep calming breath for she wanted to appear normal. There were already too many things going on and throwing another spanner in the plot would create another dimension to the ongoing story. *One thing for sure is that I won't be in Lauren's position any time soon.* Why she even thought she would amaze her. Harry and Abby had been together for over four years and had never gone down that path. She'd only been with Harry a year. *My, God, I must be losing my marbles. I'm so much in love that I want everything that life can offer Harry and me.*

As she neared Lauren, Nicky put a smile on her face in hopes that her friend wouldn't see her sorrow.

"Everything okay in there? Any blows being traded?"

"Yeah, Harry is still thankfully in one piece." Both women laughed at the joke. Nicky sat next to her friend and sipped her coffee in silence. She absently listened to Lauren and her father talk about some store in Warwick but it was all in the background as she tried to make sense of Harry's words. *Later I'll ask her and get it out in the open. Maybe Harry doesn't feel the same emotions as me. God, what a depressing thought.*

"How did it go?" Lauren asked when Harry came out of the room.

Nicky gave Harry a nonchalant glance.

"She's tired. If you want to talk with her, I suggest you go in now or she'll be asleep on you.

To most people, Harry's voice wouldn't highlight anything but to Nicky's trained ears, her lover was preoccupied.

"Thanks. Dad, you go. I want a quick word with Harry and Nicky."

"Okay, but be quick, you know how she likes her sleep."

"I'll be right there." Lauren squeezed her father's arm before he sped toward his wife.

Nicky ignored Harry's attempts to make eye contact and fixed her gaze on Steven Walker.

"Harry, are you going to stay longer now that you've met your mother?" Lauren asked.

"Actually, I'm going sooner because I *have* met my mother."

Lauren and Nicky stared at her in disbelief.

Nicky wondered what had transpired between Harry and her mother. "Sooner? I thought we were going to …"

"We were, Nicky. I need to see my uncle as soon as possible." Harry cast a concerned eye at her. "Are you okay if we go this evening?" Harry shrugged "If you'd rather, you could always stay here, and I'll pick you up on my way back?"

"No, I want to go with you."

"Will you come back here?" Lauren asked.

"Depends on what my uncle has to say for himself. It was an interesting visit, in spite of the devious way you went about arranging it."

Lauren shrugged. "Would you have done it any differently?"

"Actually, no, I wouldn't. Take care of yourself and give my regards to Maggie."

Chapter Nineteen

"Harry?"

"Yes?" Harry's mind was on her upcoming visit to her uncle and the necessary arrangements she needed to make. She failed to notice the upset inflection in Nicky's tone. "You know if we go straight to the airport I can reschedule the aircraft sooner and have Jimmy file a flight plan as soon as possible."

Harry unlocked the vehicle and opened the driver's side fully expecting Nicky to do the same. It wasn't until she slid behind the wheel and turned on the ignition that she realized her partner wasn't at her side. She turned her gaze to the woman silently standing several yards away from the car and creased her brow. Her tall frame emerged back outside and gave Nicky a quizzical stare.

"You finally remembered me."

Harry lifted an eyebrow and stroked a hand across her face. "Of course I remembered you, Nicky. What's the problem?"

"Problem? Why would there be a problem? I was just taking in the scenery."

Harry was dumbfounded at Nicky's tone and her comment but wasn't prepared to do anything but proceed with her plans. *I really don't have time for this.* "Okay, the scenery. Sure, it's a nice place. Are you going to get in the car? I want to get to the airport as soon as possible." Harry didn't have time for a hysterical outburst. Later, after the visit with her

Uncle Harry, she would clear up any misunderstanding that Nicky might have.

"I've changed my mind. I think I'll stay here with Lauren and keep her company." Nicky tried to keep her voice even. "Lauren said Maggie might not be back today. You'll be busy with your uncle so I'll just stay put until you get back."

"You're not coming?" The sudden turn of events perplexed Harry. *I would have appreciated Nicky's reassurance during the flight and with my uncle.*

"No." Nicky shrugged. "You'll come back all the sooner if you don't have to think about keeping me entertained." She walked slowly toward the car and when she reached Harry, she kissed her cheek. "See you when you get back."

For a brief moment, Harry felt that this was a permanent goodbye. *No, it can't be. There isn't any reason for me to think that way…is there?* "I love you, Nicky. I'll call when I have the flight times. Please keep your cell on."

Nicky took a step backward. "Okay, have a safe journey and don't worry, everything will be fine."

Harry eyed Nicky and desperately wanted to ask her to reconsider—she didn't. "Thanks, I'll be back sooner than you can miss me."

Harry sat back in the vehicle and revved the engine before she put it in gear and pulled out of the parking space.

∞

Lauren sat in a large overstuffed chair in the waiting room. This, of course, wasn't the room everyone used. It paid to have money. She had tried several times to reach Maggie and tell her they arrived safely but only got a generic recording. If only she could at least hear her voice then she would know everything was going to be okay. *I know deep down, that if anything happens to Maggie I'll know instantly.* Lauren's musing stopped when she saw Nicky coming toward her.

"Hey, hi. I thought you were going with Harry?"

"No, it is best if she does this on her own. It killed me to let her go but it was the right thing to do. You should have seen her face." She shook her head slightly and frowned. "It broke my heart."

"Come sit with me. I have something to tell you."

"Please, don't ask me to keep any secrets from Harry." She sat down and curled her legs under her.

"It's nothing like that at all. I wanted you to get a better look at my ring."

Nicky gazed at Lori's ring finger.

"I still can't believe that Maggie wants me as her life partner."

"It is gorgeous. I don't think I have ever seen a ring quite like this one."

"Maggie had it designed. See, these are our souls and then our hearts and then our joined souls and hearts." Lori touched each stone as she recalled Maggie's pledge to her. "She told me that when we are apart my love sustains her. I hope that is what is happening to her right now for her love is sustaining me."

"You are so lucky to have someone like Maggie in your life. It's obvious that you and Maggie have a special bond. I can see that in your ring. It's sentimental and romantic. If I had to describe Maggie in one word, romantic wouldn't come to mind." Nicky let out a half laugh.

"Oh, she is very romantic. I remember when we were here after my mother was shot and we were all tired from waiting and worrying ..."

Nicky interrupted. "Your mother was shot? When and by whom?"

"Not too long ago. That's why she's here now. She has an infection from the dialysis."

"Dialysis? Lori what does that mean, a transplant?"

"Unfortunately, yes," Lori's eyes filled with tears. "All the family members are gone so we must wait for a donor. That either means someone's life is over or some benevolent person is a match and willing to give up one of their kidneys."

"What about you, Lori? Can't you donate your kidney?"

"Not a match." A tear trickled down her cheek. "Anyway, back to my story. One of the nights, Maggie led me to a private room here in the hospital and when we got there, she had a romantic candlelight dinner for me with roses and soft music. Just what I needed then. To know I was loved." She fingered the locket around her neck.

"Hey, my friend. Where does a girl get a decent meal and a place to sleep in this town?"

Lori took her friend's hand and giggled. "Nic, I love you. Come on, I have a room reserved for you. We can order pizza and beer just like the old days.

After Lori told her parents good night and that she was leaving, the two old friends left the hospital knowing that this night they would be alone although together.

∞

The flight for Harry had been a long one. Not the actual time, but the fact that Nicky wasn't with her, made it seem like forever. Her thoughts turned morbid as she wondered what Nicky might think of her by leaving her behind in Warwick. *Things aren't quite what I originally thought they would be. In fact, they're somewhat worse than I expected.* All she had planned to do was to see Victoria, give her a hard time over abandoning her as a baby, and leave once she said her piece. The matter would be over with and she and Nicky would go home and settle down together in their new home. That had been her plan.

Against her better judgment, Harry had warmed to her mother. Even more astounding, were her feelings when Victoria spoke of Harry's father. For her, Rob Aristides, who she thought could do no wrong, sat firmly atop of a golden pedestal that was still intact although he had not been without the odd flaw or two. However, Victoria hadn't labored the point, merely glossed over them as she narrated her early life with him. When her mother took a breath after she finished her story, Harry knew it wasn't a life she would have appreciated living. To Harry, it was more of a life that Nicky might relate to since her parents lived the nomad life. Though, perhaps she would have adapted as Nicky had, but in her heart, she knew that wasn't the case. Abby had never truly settled for the life she had come to endure with her parents. It didn't suit everyone even if born into it.

The taxi pulled up outside the well kept house that her uncle had inherited from his grandmother on his mother's side when she was five years old. They had moved from a bachelor apartment to the rambling but wonderful home that was full of character. It had been a haven for her when school was out. It had a large orchard where she had spent many happy solitary hours dreaming of what it would be like to have a family. That was until recently when the family seemed to be coming out of the woodwork.

Paying the driver, she got out of the taxi holding her valise that held a few essential items. She knew she'd find her room was just as she left it so many years earlier. Her uncle had insisted that even if she no longer lived there permanently she should never feel that it wasn't her home. At the time, she had thought it sentimental hogwash. Now, she wasn't so sure.

After opening the large ornately carved door, she walked inside and put down her bag. "Uncle Harry, are you home?" The acoustics in the house traveled quite a long way. She recalled that her uncle always heard her even if she didn't want him to.

The sound of feet walking toward her on the polished wooden floor made her smile. That was her uncle all right. She would never mistake the sound of his footsteps for anyone else. He had a very distinctive sound—or was it merely familiar. She was beginning to wonder about all aspects of her life in this house and with her uncle. The main question that overrode any other —had she been happy?

A tall, very distinguished looking man who still managed to turn up with the odd pretty woman on his arm entered the room. Her uncle was the ultimate charmer and bachelor, through and through. Once she'd asked him if he ever wanted to get married and he winked and said there were too many pretty fish swimming in the sea. He didn't want to miss any of them. A selfish remark maybe, but he had always been honest with his girlfriends. They were the ones who ultimately ended the relationships when they wanted more than he could ever give to one woman. Harriet was the one constant person in his life. Though they were often apart, the time together was always fun. It was what she took back to the dorm once the vacations were over. Her roommates had always considered her uncle exciting in comparison to their boring parents. For Harriet, she wished she could trade her uncle for a boring family life often musing whether anyone was ever happy with their lot in life.

"Harriet, you look wonderful. I was half expecting you."

She smiled as she accepted his kiss on the cheek and the affectionate hug he always gave her. "Am I that predictable?"

"No, this was a special circumstance. Have you eaten? I'll have Randal make you an omelet."

Harry licked her lips at the thought and smiled. Randal, her uncle's long time valet, had a wonderful omelet recipe. "Thanks, I haven't eaten. Does he have any corn muffins to go with it?"

"For you, he will make a fresh batch if he hasn't. Give me a couple of minutes."

"Okay, I'll go up to my room and freshen up. I'll meet you in the study in ten minutes." She eyed the older man as she walked away and considered what she saw. *I wonder if he is okay. He doesn't look like his normal spry self. Maybe that is why Lori told me to visit him. I'll take a closer look when we meet later.*

A minute later, Harry looked around her room. It hadn't changed since she was last there. *How long ago was that? Too long.* She went over and opened the window, which overlooked the orchard. The view made her smile as she felt the sense of familiarity and safety settle about her. She picked up the Princess phone that adorned her nightstand for as long as she remembered and dialed Nicky's cell. There was an answer after the first ring and her smile turned into a grin.

"Hello."

"Hello yourself." Harriet's body relaxed.

"Harry, did you arrive okay?"

She heard the breathless inflection in Nicky's voice and knew that was a good omen. *She isn't upset with me after all.* "I missed you though."

There was a silence. "Is your uncle home?"

"Yeah. He's gone to ask Randal to make me one of his special omelets."

"Randal?"

"I've never mentioned him?"

"No."

"He's my uncle's valet and friend. He's always been here. He's part of the family I guess. Would you believe he was the one who got to change the diapers when I was a baby?"

Nicky laughed. "That, I would have liked to see."

"If you had, you and I would hardly be together now would we."

"Okay, point taken. Will you call me later or in the morning if it gets late?"

"I'll call you later. What are you doing for dinner?"

"Lori and I had pizza and beer after we left the hospital. Right now, I'm in my hotel room waiting for Lori to watch a movie with me."

"What movie?"

"Not sure. When she gets here we will see what is on offer then make our decision."

"Sounds like a plan." Harry looked at the clock on the dresser and realized she had told her uncle fifteen minutes ago she'd join him in ten minutes. "Nicky, I have to go. I'll call later to say good night I promise. I love you and I miss you."

"I love you too, Harry. I hope the talk with your uncle works out."

"It will. Talk with you later, bye."

Harry held the phone to her chest and felt Nicky close beside her. She took a deep breath before she left the room and headed for the study. It was going to be yet another confrontation in a day filled with conflict.

Chapter Twenty

They had discussed several subjects and avoided the one they needed air until after Randal brought in the omelet. Harry relished the omelet with all the garnishes and devoured it much to the delight of the two older men watching her. Each had a twinkle in his eyes as they exchanged knowing looks. Once Randal cleared away the dishes and left the room, it was time to broach the reason for her visit and the packages her uncle sent to her the day before.

For the second time that day, Harry asked the only question that was pertinent. "Why?"

The older man looked at his niece. "I thought it was time you knew about your mother."

"Really? Why now? There has to be a reason for your timing." She had finally said the one thing that bothered her the most. She knew Lauren had visited her uncle but was certain there was more to the story. *There has to be.*

"Call it an old man's conscience. I wanted you to know that she didn't totally forget you."

"Has anyone talked to you recently about her?"

Silver eyebrows rose. "Why are you asking?"

"Lauren, Victoria's daughter gave me your letter. I'd say that means you saw her."

"Yes, I did. She came to my door unannounced and I gave her the letter in the hope she'd go away."

"Did she?"

"Yes."

"Was that all she wanted?"

"No, she wanted to know why I never let you see the letters or packages."

"What did you tell her?" Harry could see the sadness in her uncle's eyes and her heart went out to him. Yet, she couldn't dismiss that he tried to mislead her about Lauren's visit.

"I told her what I'll tell you. I didn't want her to have anything to do with you. You were my child not hers."

"That wasn't your decision to make, Uncle Harry."

"No, I guess it wasn't."

"I met my mother for the first time today."

This time the older man moved out of his chair and stood in front of her with a look that she was sure meant disapproval. "What made you do that? Weren't the old letters and boxes enough for you?"

"I guess I went to see her in part because Lauren asked me to visit her. With your revelation, I decided it was time for me to make my own mind up about her and not let others do it for me." She eyed her uncle and thought that he looked forlorn and tired. *He's not like himself at all.*

"I see. How is Victoria?" He walked away and turned his back on her as he stared out a window.

"She's ill and in the hospital. They told me that months ago someone shot her and now she has some sort of infection that requires hospitalization."

"I suppose she told you that I'm an unfeeling bastard for not letting you have her letters and gifts over the years? I wouldn't put it past her to score a few points against me given the chance. She left you with me in the first place and gallivanted off with my brother to god knows where with little thought for you at all."

The bitterness was palatable in the air as Harriet tried to make sense of why her uncle was angry. *I'm the one that should feel aggrieved.* "She didn't say anything about you other than ask how you were doing."

"What do you think about me now that you know I deprived you of a relationship with your mother?"

Harriet stood up she walked over to stand by her uncle. In all the years she had known him, he had never sounded frightened no matter what the situation. At that moment, however, she heard the tremor that beset his voice. For years since Abby died, she'd been unable to have forgiveness as part of her repertoire but now, she was a different woman. Nicky had seen to that. Her lover's tender heart would be crying for all the wrong doings over the years and the wasted time for them all. *How different it could have been.* It was a time to forgive and move on and find a happy medium for everyone.

"At the time I'm sure you had your reasons. Why don't you tell me all about that over a scotch? Then we're going to put it in the past and see where it all goes from here. I don't confess to understanding your motives and I'm not sure that even when you fully explain them, I'll understand. Uncle Harry, you're more than just a father to me. You were my mother and father rolled into one. I'll never forget that, nor how safe you made me feel when I was living here as a child. Even when you shipped me off the boarding school, I always knew where my home was. To me, that's all that matters. I love you Uncle Harry and that is never going to change."

Her uncle didn't move and Harry wondered if he had listened to anything that she said. She heard a choked throat clear and suddenly, she was staring into the tear drenched face of the man she had never seen cry. "I didn't mean to upset you, Uncle. I guess I'd better get that scotch for us."

"No. Harriet you've changed. I expected you to be angry and not want anything to do with me again. What's happened to change you so profoundly?"

Harriet found herself engulfed in a loving hug. "Call it a special woman named, Nicky. She's changed my life in so many ways. I want to share some of my happiness with you."

For several minutes, they stood holding held each other. Then, for the first time since her arrival, Harry felt the fragility of her uncle's body. *He isn't that old is he?*

"I have much to thank your friend Nicky for. Why isn't she here with you now?" They had never really discussed her preferences. Harry felt that her uncle wasn't too happy but held back on voicing his disapproval.

"She's visiting a friend. I'll pick her up tomorrow."

"You can't stay longer?"

"Sorry, but I promise to be back next month with Nicky. You and she can get to know each other then. How does that sound?"

"It sounds good. Now, I think I'd better tell you why I didn't let you see your mother's letters and gifts."

They both sat back in their respective chairs as he began his part of the story.

"At first, it was anger. I kept thinking she would pop out of nowhere and expect me to let her have access to you. I'd brought you up and you were my daughter and I didn't want to let you go. I was going to fight for you whatever happened. I told her that but she was pigheaded and refused to believe that I would put you through a court case. She didn't know me. I wasn't like my brother. No woman was going to run rings round me. Except one and that was because I allowed it." He smiled fondly at her. "You could always twist me round your little finger." He reached over and patted Harry's arm before he got up and stood in front of her. "Victoria sent you letters at least once a month but usually more than that along with gifts too. I should have destroyed them but I couldn't. I think deep down I knew what I was doing was wrong and I convinced myself that one day, when you were older, I'd let you have everything so you could make up your own mind. Somehow that time never came around and eventually I just ignored them and put the stuff in storage."

"You were worried she would take me from you?"

"Oh, she threatened to do it and when she passed her bar exams, I thought she was going to take me to the wire. But, by then you were ten and she was involved in a serious relationship. Perhaps her perception changed. I don't know but I had legal help too and they convinced me that no judge would let her take you from me. I sent you off to school so that you could get used to living without me if things went wrong. However, I think that made the bond between us stronger. I know it did for me. I always looked forward to the times we spent together."

Harriet listened to her uncle's story and tried to understand his motives. In her heart she knew what he did was out of love. She looked at him and smiled. "So did I. We had fun, didn't we?"

"Yeah we did, my female companions were less than happy but you were the only important female in my life and always will be."

"It doesn't explain why you decided to tell me now?"

There was silence for several minutes. "I'm dying, Harriet. I have cancer. The doctors have given me about three months, maybe six if I'm lucky. I guess my philandering ways are going to have to stop now. I thought it was time that you had more family to rely on."

The shock of the announcement was hard for Harry to take since she was unprepared for it. She gave a choked cry and stood up before her uncle pulled her easily into his arms and soothed her dark hair. "I've had a wonderful life, Harriet, and more so when you came into it. How about we make the best of the time we now have left?"

The injustice of life made Harry weep for her uncle. Nicky had made her get in touch with her emotions and now that she had, they beat her up. "We will. I promise we will."

∞

The evening was emotionally draining for Harry, more than she cared to acknowledge. Life wasn't fair and she was learning that lesson once again. After Abby died, she thought she had paid the debt life often demanded of the living. Now, she once again was spiraling into the abyss of sorrow.

Harry stretched her tired body on the bed, crumpling the neatly starched coverlet below her. She closed her eyes and allowed the weariness of the last few days since Lauren Walker had dropped into her life consume her. The series of events that Lauren and her family sparked off were causing her to reevaluate her life. She thought she had covered all the angles when Nicky came into her life a year earlier and turned it upside down. Now, she had the feeling that it wasn't over. Her gut told her that there was something else sitting in wait for her around the corner baiting her to venture there and meet it face on.

She looked at the small bedside clock shaped like a castle and remembered when her uncle brought it back for her from a visit to Switzerland. She had been eight at the time and upset at him leaving her with the resident housekeeper who never smiled. Randal let it slip that the woman had a secret crush on her uncle and only joined the household in the hope that he might notice her. Fat chance of that, she was as thin as a rake and wasn't pretty. The women her uncle often brought home were all lookers. That summer was about the only time she actually approved of any of her uncle's girlfriends. The memories made her smile and grimace at how cruel she had been to the housekeeper and many of her uncle's friends. Jealousy was a trait she and her Uncle Harry shared and they were both too stubborn to talk about it.

It was funny how a small object could bring back so many memories. It made her wonder what strange and interesting tales antiques could spin if they could talk. It was almost one in the morning and that meant it was two o'clock in Warwick. Nicky had said it would be okay to call and Harry needed to hear her voice. Everything would be okay once she reconnected with Nicky.

Punching in the numbers of Nicky's cell, she waited while it rang several times. *Damn, she must be sleeping.* As she started to hang up, she heard a sleepy voice respond.

"Hello."

"Hi, did I wake you?"

"Yes. I fell asleep waiting for your call."

"I love you, Nicky." Harry pictured Nicky all tousled with her dreamy green eyes struggling to stay awake.

"Well, I'm mighty glad to hear that because I love you too. How are you?"

Harry expelled a heavy sigh. It wasn't a good time for an emotional conversation since they were both weary. All it would achieve was to upset Nicky too. "I'm okay. Not wonderful for it was an emotional evening."

"Did you have all your questions answered?"

"Yeah, I think so. Those that I could answer anyway. I think it's time to move on and forget the past and look to the future."

"I wish I was there with you. I'm sorry."

Harry blinked at the apology. "I should be the one to be apologizing. I'm so preoccupied with my own selfish agenda that I didn't consider you in all this and what you have had to put up with in the last few days."

"I heard what you said to Victoria."

"What did I say?"

"That you were alone in life and wanted it that way. I thought after all that had gone on, you wanted your old life back, and I was extra baggage."

"No. No, Nicky. How could you think that? You *are* my life and the only life I want. I would give up everything for you. Everything. I didn't want Victoria interfering with us so I said I was happy alone. As soon as I said it, and saw that you heard me, I knew I was wrong. I thought you would understand. I'm so sorry, Nicky. I didn't mean to hurt you. I love you so much that knowing I hurt you is stabbing me in the heart." Harry realized that in a few short sentences she caused a tremor in her relationship with Nicky. How life mocked her. It was punishing her for every mistake she made as she clawed to earn every scrap of love and warmth anyone gave her.

"It's okay, Harry. We're okay. I promise. You can make it up to me when we go home. How's that for a deal?"

Harry gulped back her sobs knowing that Nicky would blame herself for not being there with her. *Stupid pride.* "I love that kind of deal. I'll be back tomorrow to collect you then we can go home. Did you and Lauren have a fun night?"

"Yeah, we caught up. She told me all about Maggie's proposal. Do you know why Victoria is in the hospital?"

Harry heard the wistful note in Nicky's voice when she spoke of Lauren and Maggie's betrothal. The mention of her mother brought her back to the conversation. "Not really. I think I heard the mentioned of a virus. Why?"

"It's a bit more complicated than that."

"Complicated? Why? Is she infectious? Are we all going to come down with what she has?" A chuckle resonated down the phone line as Harry appreciated the irony of that particular situation. "That would be about right with all that's gone on before. Wouldn't it?"

"She needs a new kidney and they're struggling to find a donor. Actually it's highly doubtful they will."

133

"What do you mean doubtful? I thought there was a register for that kind of thing. It's quite a common procedure these days, isn't it?"

"She has a rare blood type. The doctors say the only viable donor is a close family member. Even then the chances are slim."

"Well, that's not a problem. Surely she has family?"

"That's just it, Harry, she doesn't. All her immediate family, bar one, is dead. There doesn't appear to be much hope."

"Lauren isn't a match then?" As she said the words, she immediately realized that her sister couldn't be a donor–she wasn't Victoria's birth child. *Even Nicky doesn't know that.* Money and power were useful at times.

"No, unfortunately she isn't."

The silence seemed endless, as the situation loomed heavy in the air.

"I'll … that is … damn."

"I understand,"

Galvanized into action, Harry leapt off the bed almost yanking the phone from the socket. "Want to meet me for breakfast in say four hours?"

"I'd love to. Where do you want me?"

Harry smiled at the double entendre and laughed. "I know where I would like you but, I guess the hospital will have to do for now. Oh, and bring along my wayward sister and her father. I think it's time they got used to having Harriet Aristides in the family and in charge, don't you?"

"Does that mean what I think it means?"

"Probably. I'll see you in four hours and remember this, Nic, I love you more every second of everyday. See you soon."

134

"Harry, will you come by here first? Please."

"Why? Is something wrong?"

"No. I just want to see you first, that's all. I need a moment alone with you. Do you mind?"

"Not at all. The hotel it is and then we'll gather my family together." Harry let her eyes rest on the clock again. "If I'm going to get there I'd better set things in motion. See you soon."

Chapter Twenty-one

She tossed and turned as the dream of a dark object, with no means of escape, ran for its life. She cried out trying to warn the object of the danger as hideous wolves and jackals came from all angles ready to attack and make the kill. The object kept running toward something but she couldn't see what. The sheets were wet with perspiration as she tried in vain to help. *Why can't I help?* Terror for the object filled her for she could see there was no escape or hope. Then, she saw it and trembled at the evil she felt. In the shadows, lurking was a dark hulking figure, weapon pointed and ready to fire. "No," she screamed. "Run, run faster and get away." Then an arrow sailed and she knew its path was true.

Lauren woke with a start. "Maggie?" The incessant knocking on the door caught her attention. "Be right there." She struggled to free herself from the wet tangle of sheets.

She's back already. A bright smile filled her face. When she opened the door, she was crestfallen and her heartbeat quickened as she struggled to breathe. "What are you doing here?" was all she could manage before she lost consciousness.

∞

Harry jabbed the elevator button decisively. She was bone tired. Her travels to Texas and back along with the emotional roller coaster of the last twenty-four hours were almost more than she could bear. At the same time, she was happy to be there. The next stop the elevator made would be on Nicky's floor.

Harry leaned her exhausted body against the wall of the elevator and she closed her eyes. She wondered what Nicky would say to her. More to the point, what would she say to Nicky? Things definitely needed airing. She didn't want to go into the operating room leaving any doubts in Nicky's mind as to how she felt. She knew the chances of anything going wrong during the operation were slim, but she had to make her peace with the only person, other than her Uncle, that she loved. Her trip to Galveston took care of her Uncle for the time being and soon she'd be in Nicky's arms.

A bleep woke her from her meandering thoughts and she straightened up as she waited for the door to open. Once they glided back with a sleek mechanical sound she stepped out and scanned the wall across from her for the direction of Nicky's room. She proceeded left down a silent corridor. It was only six in the morning and not too many were out of bed.

It didn't take too long for her to be in front of Nicky's door. She lightly tapped on the door and when Nicky didn't come to the door, she knocked harder. Nicky would probably be in a grouchy mood since she loved her sleep. Harry chuckled as she recalled the number of occasions that she had to drag her out of bed or they would be late for work. Of course, once she was awake, Nicky's idea of being late for work was very pleasurable.

The door cracked open and a bleary eyed woman peered at her in confusion. Then Nicky was miraculously alive and in her arms.

"Whoa, Nic, let me in the room first?" Harry felt her heart jump in reaction as she hugged Nicky. She was grateful and never wanted Nicky to leave her. *The pain would be even greater than when I lost Abby.* She had only admitted that the night before when she talked with her uncle.

"Oh, Harry, I'm so glad you're back." The kisses they then shared were so feverish that it gave the impression they hadn't seen each other for ages.

"Would you mind if I used the bathroom? I'm kind of desperate."

"I'm sorry." Nicky reluctantly released Harry. "Do you want coffee or anything?"

"Nope, I'm fine. I've had as much coffee as I need. Too much probably. When all this is over, I'm going to have caffeine withdrawal,"

Harry returned from the bathroom and saw a strange look on Nicky's face. "Is everything okay?"

"Have we time to talk?" Nicky asked.

"Absolutely, that's why I'm here." As soon as she said the words, Harry realized how dumb they sounded. As a shuttered look came over Nicky, she sighed. *Christ, won't I ever learn?*

Harry removed her jacket and slipped out of her slacks and shoes so quickly that Nicky hadn't noticed. Then Harry gathered her into a warm embrace and pulled her gently onto the bed. "I want to talk with you too, Nicky. I never want to go away again as I did yesterday with any misunderstanding between us. It breaks my heart."

"There wasn't any misunderstanding, Harry. You did what you had to do." Nicky snuggled into the loving embrace.

Harry pulled Nicky closer and kissed the top of her head. Her need to become as close to her lover and melt into her was overwhelming. Harry breathed in the scent of the early morning. It was the in-between odor of the shower the night before, perspiration emitted during the night and the natural smell of the person she loved. Her lover's essence drew Harry closer as she blew out a breath. "I know I ask a great deal of you, Nicky, and I'm sure I won't change much over the years. Please remember this, I love you beyond reason, you are my life." With those words, Harry placed another stake in the ground that defined her relationship with Nicky.

Overwhelmed, Nicky gulped back the happy tears. "As you are mine. I know you wanted to go to the hospital immediately but I needed to hold you and show you that I'll be here with you whatever you decide to do."

Harry smiled and placed her lips on the Nicky's soft hair. She trusted Nicky to be there whatever circumstances came their way. Even if she, at times, had a hard time believing it could be true that someone could and would love her so much they put their own feelings to the background if necessary.

However, was that the right thing to do? She'd berated herself enough over her own selfish needs wanting something she knew, at least thought she knew, wasn't possible—unwavering love. Why did she want that kind of commitment from Nicky? She'd asked herself a million times returning the same verdict—uncertainty. Yes, it probably stemmed from her background and the fact that though her Uncle loved her dearly, he was never there for all the scrapes, bumps and bruises she had as a child growing up. Yes, she'd said to her Uncle Harry that he was her father and mother rolled into one and she meant every word. Yet, she'd needed something he hadn't been able to give her, and now when she thought of Lauren she was jealous. Jealous that the younger woman had received the attention she had not from their shared parent.

"I've decided to help Victoria. I'll have the test to see if I'm donor compatible."

"And, if you are?"

"Then I guess we will be staying a little longer than we planned. I'll have Sally cancel my schedule for the short term."

Nicky moved on top of Harry and grinned. "Will that mean I receive time off to take care of a sick loved one?"

Harry chuckled as she imagined Nicky as her nurse. That sent a sexual shiver down her spine but she knew it wasn't the right time for that. "I think it could be arranged with the boss."

Nicky kissed Harry so passionately that for a few moments, her lover forgot exactly why she was there. "I love you, Harriet."

"I love you, Nicky, more than you will ever know. I've never loved anyone so deeply." A sharp intake of breath from Nicky caused Harry to frown. "Nic, is there a problem? Are you okay?"

"No problem, I'm good, I promise." When we get home can you say that to me again, please?"

"For you anything, anyplace, anywhere, anytime."

"How I love you, Harry," Nicky said. "I wish I could stay in your arms forever."

Harry chuckled softly.

"I guess we need to go see Lauren and then onto the hospital."

"Yeah, I suppose so."

"What's wrong, Harry. I've lived with you long enough to hear the tone that says you agree with me but …"

"But. You're right, it's a big *but*, and I wish it wasn't. Before I say anymore, I want to apologize for not sharing some of my earlier life with you. Especially the time I had with my uncle."

"It's okay, it doesn't matter. We all have secrets and given time I expect I would have met him."

For a moment, Harry stared at Nicky, perplexed at how easy it was to talk with her and her acceptance of all her faults and she had many. "It does matter, Nicky. Although it's water under the bridge, I can't take back the past. I'm looking to the future and if I know you're there alongside me I can face the trials that are ahead."

"I'll be there and we will work out whatever comes our way together."

"Uncle Harry is dying, Nicky. I needed to tell you so there weren't any more secrets between us."

Nicky's face puckered in sadness as she held Harry's hand. "I promise I'm here with you no matter what the circumstances."

Harry buried her head in Nicky's shoulder as a sob escaped before she began crying for her uncle. He was the only parent she had ever known, she loved him, and she would miss him deeply. "I need you," Harry cried.

Nicky held Harry while she cried. "I'll always be here for you."

Several minutes later, Harry lifted her head and wiped away her tears. "I guess we better go see if we can wake Lor ... my sister up?"

"You know Lori hates to be disturbed when she's sleeping."

Grateful for the change of subject, a brighter smile creased Harry lips. "Strange, I know someone else like that as well."

Nicky laughed and gave Harry a wink. "Want to share my shower?"

"Try and stop me." With arms around each other, they headed for the bathroom, knowing that together they were stronger and as long as that remained, they were invincible.

∞

The woman opened the door and murmured, "No," before she collapsed into the man's arms. With great care, he picked her up and carried her to her bed. As he sat next to her, he stroked her hair and whispered soothing words.

"Get your hands off my sister," a voice demanded.

"Ah, Ms. Aristides, we meet again," the man said.

"Resnik, what are you doing here?" Harry glared daring him to touch Lauren again.

Resnik stood. "Nice to see you again, Ms. Aristides. And you are, Nicky, right?" He held his hand out.

Irritated by Resnik's condescending attitude, Harry moved between him and Nicky. "You leave her out of this. What are you doing here?"

Nicky touched Harriet's arm. "Harry, give him a chance to explain. I'll check on Lori." She moved past the other two and crawled in next to her friend stroking her face gently. "Lori, wake up."

Harry pushed past Resnik and stood next to the bed. "Do you know what's wrong with her?"

"I believe she has fainted."

With her eyes filled with fire, Harry went toe to toe with Resnik. "Believe me when I tell you, Resnik, that if you had anything to do with this you'll be sorry." Despite her bravado, Harry was trembling inside—the man scared her.

Lori began to come around. "Hey there, are you feeling okay?" Nicky asked. "That's it, Lori, open your eyes."

Harry turned back toward the bed and let out the breath she was holding as she saw Lauren's eyes open fully. "Is she all right?"

Lauren smiled as she looked at her friend by her side. "Nicky, what are you doing here?" When her eyes rested on her sister, her smile broadened. "I thought you were in Texas." She ran her fingers through her hair. "I must be a sight."

Horror replaced her smile as saw her gaze fix on Resnik.

Harry glared at Resnik. "You will regret whatever you did to her. That is a promise." She looked at her sister whose eyes welled with tears before they began trickling down her cheeks.

"No. No, it can't be. Please don't let it be. She is my life." Lauren began crying in deep heart wrenching sobs.

As she listened to her sister cry, it dawned on Harry what was happening. She turned to Resnik in understanding. "Is she?"

Patrick shook his head. "No, but it was a close call." He moved past Harry and knelt down beside the bed. "Lauren, listen to me. She is injured but safe."

It took some time for his words to register but when they did, Lauren shot up. "I must go to her."

Resnik placed his hand on her shoulder held her back "No, not now. She's at our retreat in Maryland. The best doctors we have are treating her. Right now, she needs to rest and mend."

"The hell I won't, Patrick."

"You can't go there now. It's not possible."

Lauren gave him a long hard look before she pushed his hand away and sat up. "Try and stop me."

"Lori, you can't go now," a voice from the doorway commanded.

Lauren looked past the others and saw her father standing in the doorway with a stricken look on his face. "Daddy, is it Mother?"

Steven just stood there, shaking as tears rolled down his cheeks. "You better come with me to the hospital now, sweetheart. There's not much time." It was then that he noticed Harry. "Harriet, she will want to see you too. Come with us please."

For a minute, Harry took stock and collected her thoughts in an orderly fashion—it was time to take charge. "Let's go now," she ordered.

"Can you give me a minute to get dressed?" Lauren quickly got off the bed.

"Five minutes, Lori. We will wait for you in the hallway." Harry turned and exited the room expecting the others to follow her—they did.

Outside the door, Harry eyed Lauren's father. She wanted and needed the answers only he could give. "Steve, will you please tell me what the doctors said exactly? What is the time frame here?" Nicky was at her side giving her the strength she would need if her plan was to work.

"He said every minute counted. That she could last the night or pass quickly."

"What exactly is the problem, other than the kidney? It's important to know."

"The infection is running rampant and they can't seem to stop its progress. They have run out of options." Tears once again welled in his eyes.

Harry turned to Nicky. "Do you think there's a chance your parent's new drug would work for her?"

Nicky paused when Lauren came out of her room. "Yes, I think there is a very good chance."

"A good chance for what?" Lauren asked.

"Lori, you know about my parent's new discovery."

Lauren nodded.

"I think it will work for your mother and help her get better."

Lauren nodded. "Yes, I think it is worth the risk. Daddy, she's out of options, isn't she?"

"Yes," Steve said.

"Then let's go for it, Nicky. We need to check with the doctors of course, I'm not sure they'll approve. Nicky, do you have any data we can give them?"

"Don't worry; I'll have all the information the doctors will need. In fact, I will give my mom and dad a call and get their opinion."

"Good, there is one problem though," Harry said. "The meds are in Houston and we need to get them here fast. We need at least three hours to accomplish that. Do we have that much time?" Harry shrugged. "I'm not sure any of us are willing to take that chance."

"I can help with that, Ms. Aristides. When you've decided what you need let me know and I will make some calls and it will be arranged in a matter of minutes." Resnik leveled his gaze on Harry.

Harry doubted his words. "Oh, really? Just how will you do that?"

"I have my ways, Ms. Aristides." He turned to Lauren and put his arm around her. "It will all work out, I promise."

"If only ...," Lauren said.

Patrick handed Lauren his cell phone. "Take this. After you have seen to your mother press one and she will answer."

"She knows what is happening here?" Lauren asked.

"Yes, she knows in her heart as you know in yours." He turned to the others. "I'll be leaving you now."

"If you leave, just how am I supposed to get in touch with you, Mr. Resnik or is it Sullivan?" Harry refused to buy the man's line anymore.

Again, a small smile was evident. "You don't. I call you." Then he seemed to disappear.

Chapter Twenty-two

"I have a car waiting for us," Steve noted as they exited the hotel.

The short drive to the hospital was one of reflection for all in the car.

Harry's mind was in *get things done* mode trying to figure all the angles and pitfalls. "Nic, do you need me to contact the office for any data?"

Nicky shook her head. "I'm pretty much up to date on most things except if there's been any change in the last month or so."

"You'd best call your parents when we get to the hospital."

Nicky squeezed Harry's hand. "I was thinking that very thing. Not that I want to say this in public but we did try a crude model of the formula on a native boy and he responded well."

Harry watched Lauren finger the phone. "I'm sure Maggie is going to be okay."

Lauren nodded then gazed at Harry with a wide eyed expression. "This is our mother at deaths door and I'm scared."

Harry cleared her throat. "Your dad needs support right now, he looks spaced out to me."

Lauren glanced at her dad. "I don't think he'll know what to do if anything happens to her."

Harry frowned. She'd been there before and worn that particular t-shirt and didn't want to try it on for size again anytime soon. "Victoria is a strong woman she'll pull through." Harry turned to look out the window. What she saw there was a barren wasteland and that didn't improve her mood any.

∞

The car pulled up to the hospital entrance and all silently got out and went inside. The elevator ride to the third floor was equally quiet.

As they entered the intensive care area, all eyes turned toward them. The grief on their faces told the story. They all closed in on the room, which was now familiar territory to them.

Lauren and her father entered the room that seemed filled with more machines. Once they were position next to the bed, each took one of her hands. Victoria looked very peaceful laying there with the only hint of how serious her condition was the constant beep of the monitors.

"How I wish this could be different, Lori." Steven said. "She has been my dream girl for as long as I can remember. This can't be happening. It just can't."

Lauren walked around the bed and put her hand over her father's hand. "Daddy, there is still hope. If we give up now then we should go out and start digging her grave." Her voice was strong and steady. "I am not ready to do that, are you?"

Steven looked at his daughter. "When did you grow up and become so wise, Lori?" For the first time in what seemed like days, he smiled. "You are right, sweetheart. If we give up, then what reason does she have to fight?" He looked around the room. "What happened to your sister and Nicky? They were right behind us. Weren't they?"

"I am sure they will be along in a moment. They probably wanted to give us some time alone." Lauren leaned into her father as they both watched Victoria breathe. "Her breathing is not labored, Daddy, that's a good sign."

∞

Harry held back before going in to see Victoria. She had another strategy on her mind and gently clasped Nicky's shoulder preventing her from following Lauren into her mother's room.

Quizzical eyes looked up. "Is everything okay?"

"Yes, why do you ask?" Harry's mind was on the problems at hand and the comment surprised her.

"Shouldn't we be in there with them for support?"

"We will, I promise. Why don't you call your parents? You can use my cell. They might advise us if the drug will be of any benefit or merely a hindrance. I don't want to push something that might end up being worse for Victoria." Harry pulled at her bottom lip gently in contemplation of her actions. If anything went wrong, people would misconstrue her motives and she didn't want that grievance hanging over her head.

"Sure, I'll ask at the desk where I can use a cell. If I recall some of the notes, they made on initial investigation, I think it might be what we're looking for, Harry. We have to think positive at times like this."

Harry smiled at the petite woman who, in such a small frame, gave her strength that constantly amazed her. Nicky was one woman you could never underestimate in anyway. It was Harry's good fortune to be on the receiving end of such a loving package. She intended to remain that way for the rest of their lives.

"I love you, Nicky, did I ever tell you that?" A beaming smile flashed over her lover's face bringing a ray of sunshine into an otherwise dark start to the day.

"Yeah, but it's always wonderful to hear it. By the way, I love you too. I'll be back as soon as I can. Go inside and see her, Harry. They all need you."

Harry opened her mouth to say more but a finger gently closed her partially open lips.

"Go, Harry, it's the right thing to do." Nicky departed the area as she made for the nurse's station.

Harry closed her eyes briefly as a wave of emotion overcame her. She gulped in a deep breath and made every effort to be strong for the others in the room the door she now faced. She knew that when she needed to call on her support it would be there at her side in the shape of Nicky. *How lucky did I get to have two women love me in my lifetime?* When all this was over, she would let Nicky know exactly how much she meant to her.

∞

The door opened and Harry strode in as if she was squaring up for a boardroom battle rather than fighting for someone's life. "How is she?"

Lauren and Steven turned toward the voice.

Frustrated at the lack of communication from the father and daughter act in front of her, Harry cleared her throat. "Okay, have you talked with the doctor yet?"

"Right now she is holding her own, Harry. Why not come over here with me?" Lauren held out her hand.

"Harry, the doctor is on his way." Steve said. "We wanted you and Nicky here with us. It's a decision we all should make together."

Harry frowned as she tried to reconcile exactly what the outstretched hand meant. A link to a family she didn't know existed until recently. What were they offering her? She didn't understand this gesture and she wished that Nicky were here with her to help her decide what to do.

"Harry, I am not going to bite," Lauren said.

"I know and if you did, you'd find me as tough as old boots." Harry tried to inject a little humor into a situation that made her nervous. "Nicky is making a call to her parents and she'll be back shortly."

"Good. Then the timing should be about right." Lauren dropped her hand.

Harry was looking around the room in every place but one—the bed that held the woman who was dying. A part of her wanted to act as if this was a stranger and it didn't matter. However, a primal emotion deep inside her gut told her that wasn't going to happen and she wanted to run away and hide.

"Uhmm, why don't I go to see what is keeping Doctor Green" Steve said.

"Good idea, Steve. Want me to come with you?"

"Harry, what is the matter? This is your mother and not some stranger off the streets.

Why am I behaving like a coward? Harry had never run away from anything before in her life. Here she was sprinting away instead of facing the fact that this woman had given birth even if she hadn't stuck around to see her grow up. Galvanized into meeting the challenge of Lauren's words, Harry focused on why she was there. "Nothing is wrong and I know who she is." Harry moved alongside Lauren and stared down at her mother.

"Look, Harry, I know this is difficult for you. We mean you no harm. Mom just wanted to see you and know you were okay. That's all. I think she knew she was dying."

"Yes, it is difficult. You're a doctor, Lauren. You come across sick people all the time. I do not. Frankly, the last time I was in a hospital was to say goodbye to someone I loved. Does that answer your question?" Harry tried to shake off the memory of going to the hospital morgue to identify Abby's body.

Lauren looked at Harry. "Do you really think that seeing our mother laying here, perhaps gasping her last breath is easy for me? Yes, I have seen death, but I promise you, it is never easy no matter how detached you try to be. Yes, we handle it differently. Nevertheless, my heart has bled for every one of my patients, Harry. I need some air." Lauren turned to leave the room.

Harry knew she was digging a big hole for herself and wished Nicky was by her side to soothe the ache she felt. "Please, don't go." This time Harry held out her hand in a gesture she wasn't entirely sure about but it somehow seemed right.

Lauren turned and smiled as she walked up to Harry and took her hand. "Hey, do you realize we've had our first sister fight?"

"Really? Is that what they call it? I wouldn't like to get into too many of those before breakfast."

Lauren smiled. "Come on, let's say *hi* to our mother."

"Okay, I can do that." Harry felt the weight she had been carrying lift slightly. It wasn't gone, but she was making headway.

"How about we agree not to fight again? This is very difficult for us all, but, as I said to my dad earlier, we cannot give up hope. Right now that's all we have."

"A truce it will be, Lauren. Can I mention one thing about me though?"

"Certainly anything."

"I never give up. It's in the blood.

"Yes, she bred fighters."

"I do believe you might be right." Unaware, Harry clasped Lauren's hand tighter in response to the emotion that created inside of her.

Arm in arm they stood by the side of the bed watching their mother, knowing she too would not give up without one hell of a fight.

∞

Nicky was in a small annex next to the main building of the hospital where she was assured that her cell would work. As she pressed the address menu, she wondered where Harry would keep the phone number. Would it be under personal or business? *Harry would file it under both.*

Once she located the code, she punched in the three digits and waited, fervently hoping that the connection would be good and that one of her parents was in the camp.

"Mom, am I glad to be speaking with you."

"Darling, how wonderful. I wasn't expecting a call from you for at least another week or two. Is everything okay?" Her mother's jolly rejoinder was a breath of fresh air that Nicky needed.

"Yes, well no, not exactly. Harry's mother is critically ill and is in the hospital. I was wondering …"

"I didn't know Harry had a mother. Well, you know what I mean, darling."

"Yeah, yeah I know what you mean, Mom, and yes she does. It's a long story and I want to tell you all about it but I haven't the time right now but I'll fill you in later. The new drug, Mom, you used it on that native boy didn't you? I saw it in your files. Why did you do that?"

There was a brief silence. "It was a long shot, Nicky. The boy was dying, and his father allowed us to try whatever we could. We ran out of options with conventional medicines and the only thing we had left was the new drug. Your father was cautious, and rightly so. It could have killed him. Fortunately, for us, it didn't and we went on to prove it would be of use to the world. Why do you ask?"

"Mom, Victoria, Harry and Lauren's mom, needs that chance now. I want to …

"Lauren's mom? Your friend from college?"

"Yes, look, Mom, I'll explain everything when I have the time. Would you please send your notes to Harry's private email right now? If I need you to talk with a doctor or two can you stick around near the phone for the next couple of hours?"

"I will, darling. However, please ensure that only the minimum people know what you are planning to do. Newspaper reporters have a tendency to pick up on these things and that might jeopardize the program altogether."

"Yes, I know things can be misconstrued. Everything will be okay. I promise."

"I take it Harry approves of this. What about Lauren? Is there a husband in all this?"

"Mom, of course Harry and Lauren approve. It was Harry's idea and Lauren was quick to go along with it. Don't you remember that she's a medical doctor, Mom? Lauren's father is here and I think he approves."

"Think? Nicky really. Have you girls taken control? Doesn't the man have a say in his wife's treatment? Wouldn't it be wise to gain his complete approval as well?"

"Mom, I think you have it all wrong. Look, I need to go. The cell is bleeping and probably needs a charge. Will you send the data please?"

"Yes. And, Nicky, please make sure you all know what you are doing before you mention the drug to the authorities in the hospital. Not everyone has your faith in its properties."

"I will. I promise. Love you, Mom, bye for now."

"Love you too, darling, bye."

The connection ended just as the cell's energy level hit zero. Nicky was confident that her mom would come up with the goods. However, her warnings about being cautious were valid and she would explain that to Harry and Lauren. Had they taken over control from Steven? Maybe, but it was for a good reason. Perhaps she would have a chat with him when she got back to the hospital room. *Yes, that's what I'll do.* "Now, down to action. Hopefully Harry brought her laptop. She never travels without it. I hope that is true today."

Nicky met Steven in the corridor as she headed back to Victoria's room.

"Steven, I just spoke with my mother about the drug and I think we all need to met and discuss what to do. If that's okay with you, of course."

Steven's face brightened as he spoke to the young woman whom he always admired for her gentle, kind ways. "Nicky, of course it's okay with me. I appreciate all you're doing to help my wife. What do you say we find Lori and Harry and go into the private waiting room? I will leave a message at the desk for Doctor Green to meet us there."

Nicky took his arm and guided him to Victoria's room "Actually I think we need to discuss this amongst ourselves first. There are some consequences we should consider."

Steve wiped a hand across his craggy features. "Sure, whatever you say." He blinked in amazement when he saw Harry and Lauren holding hands at Victoria's bedside.

When Steve left the room, it was the last thing to expect to see. Harriet was far too cold and withdrawn to respond to the gentle gesture of support from his daughter. Yet now, it would appear she had. *Wonders never cease.*

Lauren looked at them and smiled. "Hey, you two, I think she's coming around."

They rushed over to the bedside and a quiet hush came over them all as Victoria stirred before opening her eyes.

"Great news, Lauren." Nicky patted her friend's arm. She placed her hand into Harry's free one and squeezed it gently. "How are you doing?"

"I'm doing okay. How did the call to your parents go?"

At first, Victoria looked quizzical, and then managed a small smile for the sight of her family standing by her bedside. She tried to speak but her mouth was so dry she could not.

Lauren bent down. "Welcome back, Mom. Do you want a drink of water?"

Victoria nodded.

"Is the doctor coming, Steven?" Harry asked.

Steven looked at Nicky then Harry. "Nicky, didn't you say we need to discuss this before we talk with the doctor?"

"Nicky, is it a possibility?"

"Mom is downloading her data to your personal email. She had a warning that I thought we need to discuss between us before we involve the doctors."

"Yes, I think we do and I think we should involve Victoria in the conversation and decision." All eyes turned to Steven in surprise. "It is her life after all."

"Nicky, what are you talking about? What warning?" Lauren asked.

"I was talking with my mother and she said we had to be very sure about who we are involving in this discussion. If the news gets out that we are proposing to use a new untested drug, it could have serious consequences for us all—but mainly Victoria."

"Nicky's right, we need to play this hand close to our vests," Harry said.

"Yes, I understand that point of view, Nicky. If we involve Doctor Green in using an untested drug, he could lose his license. We need to make sure we make the right decision about this. I think we need to speak with Mom so she understands all that is happening."

"I think Nicky and Lauren should explain this from their different points of view," Steven said.

"You better start with the basics, Nicky."

"Victoria, you have an infection that at the moment is sapping all your energy. The doctors are trying to find medication to help you however, they are having little success."

"I'm dying, aren't I?"

A sharp cough reverberated around the room as Steven moved closer to the bed and held his wife's hand giving them both comfort. "Sweetheart, we have run out of options. There doesn't seem to be anywhere to turn but there is one option."

"Victoria, you've been a sick woman for some time now and this isn't helping the matter. Harry and I thought we might have a solution."

"Harry, is she here?"

"I'm here." Harry replied.

"Harry, you came back. Did you even leave me? I thought it was a figment of my fevered imagination that you were standing beside Lauren as I always hoped you would one day."

"Yes, I came back to you. I can't let my mother have anything but the best possible shot, can I?"

Victoria smiled and reached for Harry. "Thank you." She cried. "I'm so sorry, Harry, that our time is so short. I'm afraid my body and soul are too weak to go on."

Harry replied, "I don't give up and I'm not giving up on you now that I've found you."

Nicky said, "We're working on a new drug that my parents found in the Amazon jungle. It's experimental and is in its infant stage but my mother once used it on a native boy who was beyond the help of conventional drugs. We thought perhaps ..."

Steven moved closer to his wife. "Darling, I think we need to consider this alternative. If we don't I'm afraid there is nothing else to be done."

"Yes." Victoria slipped back into sleep.

Just then, Harry's other cell rang. "Sorry, I'll be right back."

∞

Once Harry was in the stairwell and out of the telemetry range, she flicked open, her phone.

"Ms. Aristides, can you have your people go to the airport with the drug?" Harry knew the voice. It was Resnik.

"Yes, they can be there within fifteen minutes of my call."

"Good, have them go to hanger twenty-two and Colonel Collins will meet them there and take charge of the drugs. He will then arrive at the hospital within an hour and a half. I have arranged for the local police to meet him and deliver him to the hospital."

The man of mystery took Harry aback somewhat. "You certainly know how to get things done. Care to share your secrets?"

"No."

The connection was lost.

Harry, stunned by the call, let out a low whistle. "Wow, I wish he worked for me."

∞

Lauren, watched her mother sleep, turned a tear stained face to Nicky. "Where is Harry?"

"She had to take a call," Nicky said.

"I see. I am sure it was important."

Nicky was trying desperately to take Lauren's mind off the fact that Harry had left so suddenly. Harry had told her that Sally was blocking all calls to her cell.

"Why don't you explain what this might mean to your father on a personal front?" Nicky wanted to be sure that everyone understood exactly what was at stake. "I'll go find out where Harry went while you talk with your dad. Okay?"

"Thank you, Nicky. Dad, this drug is untested. What does that mean? She could die from the medication or she could completely recover. We have no way of knowing. The fact that it is untested means there can be a multitude of side effects that we know nothing about. When the word experimental is used, it means every aspect of the word. There will be no guarantees." She paused.

Just as Nicky was about to leave the room, she saw a pained look on her friend's face and turned her attention to the direction Lori was looking. When she saw Steven face pale under his tan she remembered her mother's words. *Instead of telling him what we are going to do we need his input.*

"Are you okay with this, Dad? If there is any doubt at all we will not proceed and just let nature takes its course."

"Mr. Walker, your opinion about what we should do is important. The last thing we want to do is railroad you into a choice you do not want," Nicky said.

"I know, Nicky, and thank you."

Harry entered the room.

Steven turned and smiled. "Glad you came back."

"I'm sorry I had to leave that call was important. Have you arrived at a decision? The drug is on its way here."

Steven cleared his throat. "I think it is wise to keep what we are doing between us." He looked at his daughter. "We can administer it ourselves can't we, Lori?"

"Yes, Daddy, we can and I will do it."

The abrupt nature of Harry's announcement perturbed Nicky. *She isn't asking them she is telling them.* "You fully understand what that means to you and your career?"

"Yes, I understand completely, Nicky. Of course, the final decision is up to my dad."

"No, sweetheart, it is up to your mother."

"We shall ask her when she wakes then." Lauren kissed her mother's cheek.

With difficulty, Victoria opened her eyes. "Baby, I heard what you said. Please don't blame yourself if anything goes wrong. This is my decision to go ahead with this. I love you for being here for me." Victoria clutched Steve's hand "Darling, I have always loved you. Harry, I love you, I always have and always will. I'm so sorry it took this long to find you. Please forgive me." She closed her eyes once more.

Nicky watched the family and wondered if Harry knew what she was risking. Then chastised herself. *Of course, Harry knows.* She would lose a great deal if this went wrong. Her mother probably, and Harry would have to give up her position as head of the company. After all, she agreed to disregard all the rules and protocols to get the drug so they could use it. *One thing I know for sure, I'm going to be at her*

*side and that is all that matters to me I just hope it's
enough for her.*

Chapter Twenty-three

The medication was on its way and Lauren, having to wait for it, collapsed into a soft chair while taking the cell phone out of her pocket. She really needed to call Eden Martin but that had to wait until she heard Maggie's voice. Pressing the number, she waited to hear the sound that would make everything right again.

A weak voice answered. "Lauren is that you?"

"Yes."

"It is so good to hear your voice."

"Maggie, I have been so worried about you. Please tell me what happened."

"I'm going to be fine, Lauren. Don't worry about me you have enough to be concerned with there."

To Lauren, Maggie's voice sounded strained and her breathing harsh. "I worry about you, Maggie, that's what I do. Now, please, tell me."

"Okay, I will try. After I was certain you were all on board and your plane had taken off, I went to the police station. Unfortunately, they allowed Tommy to have his phone call and he called his boss, Lester."

"He's the one that tried to kill you, isn't he?"

"Yes. Anyway, after Rick, one of my dad's men, and I convinced Tommy to tell us where we could find Lester I went there to have it out with him once and for all." Maggie went silent for a few seconds then began again. "The area was out in a remote part of the town surrounded by trees and big boulders. It was a set up, Lauren. Lester and his men were waiting for me. Do you want me to continue or stop?"

"No, please continue. I want to know everything." Lauren needed to hear it all before she could continue with the trial facing her later.

"Okay, but you stop me if you've heard enough."

"I will. Please continue."

"I felt the first bullet before I heard it. It grazed my head and as with all head wounds, it bled profusely. I couldn't see out of my right eye. I crawled behind a rock and tore my shirtsleeve to make a bandage for my head. I didn't have much time though. I heard someone coming behind me and I turned and shot him but he got one off and it hit me in the chest." Again, she paused. "I rolled over, spotted another of Lester's men, and shot him. Then I got to my feet and started to look around for the rest but another shot rang out and hit my left thigh. I collapsed to the ground and when I looked up, Lester was standing over me pointing his gun at my head. He had a sneer on his face and told me I would pay for killing his brother." She cleared her throat.

"Lauren, at that point all I could do was to try and figure out how to get away from him and come back to you. At that moment, I knew you and I would always be together, even in death. I told Lester to go ahead but he hesitated long enough to tell me he would be looking you up to kill you too. I tried to get up but he kicked me down breaking my collarbone. He cocked the trigger. The next thing I knew his face filled with horror and he fell over on me and there was an arrow was protruding from his back. I must have passed out because when I opened my eyes next I was in the safe house hooked up to all kinds of monitors with my father standing next to the bed."

The silence from Lauren was deafening. "That's all there is to tell. I've been stitched up, have a tube in for my collapsed lung, and I have bandages everywhere."

Lauren shook. "You're alive, that is what is important, Maggie. I'm grateful for whoever finished Lester off."

"No one knows who shot the arrow. As for Lester, he is still alive but just barely. They have him in a secure facility."

Lauren could not stop the flow of tears coursing down her cheeks. "I need you."

"I know. I will be there as soon as I can arrange for a helicopter to pick me up." She quickly wrote a note and handed it to her aid so she could be on her way.

"So much has happened. I don't know if I can do what I need to, Maggie."

"Lauren, you can do what you have to, because you must. You are your mother's only hope. I will be there as soon as I can. Until then, whenever you feel any doubt just touch your locket and I will be there with you."

"You know?"

"Yes, my father told me. I need to go now and get some things together so I will be ready to leave. You'll get a message about my arrival time."

"Goodbye, Maggie. I love you."

"Love you too. Bye.

∞

Nicky walked into the waiting room and noticed Lori, sitting and holding a phone close to her heart. "Hey, you okay?"

Lauren smiled. "Yeah, I'm fine. I need to speak with your mother. Do you have the number handy?"

"Sure, I can give you the number, Lori. Before you call her, you need to look at the data she sent. It may answer some of your questions and also help you ask more informed questions."

"I'd prefer talking to her, Nicky, and not read field notes."

"Hey, I didn't mean that you shouldn't speak with my mother. I just thought you might like to look at her notes first. I have Harry's laptop and have cued the documentation if you want to take a look."

"Nicky, I'm sorry for sounding ungrateful. I will read the reports before I speak with your mother." She sighed heavily. "I just spoke with Maggie."

Nicky sat down next to her. "How is she?"

"I'm not sure. She wanted me to think what happened to her was no big deal, but I know it wasn't."

"What happened to her?"

"She was in an accident and her injuries are significant."

"Oh, Lori, how awful. Is she going to be okay?"

"She told me she's on her way here. From a medical standpoint, I know she is not strong enough for travel, but I need her with me. If I were her doctor I'd forbid her from leaving the hospital." Lauren rubbed her face. "I'm being selfish and need to call her back and tell her not to come. That would be the wise thing to do. But at the moment, I'm not feeling very wise."

"Lori, why not let this burden be handled by Maggie's doctors. Let them decide if she can travel or not. Right now, you need to concentrate on the drug that could save your mother's life."

"I'm scared, Nicky."

Nicky placed a comforting arm around Lauren's shoulders and pulled her closer. "I know you are, Lori. Who wouldn't be? I can't imagine what you must be going through right now. What can I do to help you?"

Lori smiled. "Just being here with me is a comfort, Nicky. Thank you. I wish ..."

"You wish? If I can grant it, I will."

"I want Harry to understand what all this means, not only to me, but to her too. I don't think she is feeling anything. It seems to me that the logistics of getting the drug here is all she cares about."

Nicky's scowled. *You really have no idea how cut up she is Lori and I can't let you into that secret place.* "She does care. You'll have to take my word on that."

"In my line of work I've seen too many people regret not sharing their emotions while a loved one was still living. I don't want that for Harry. "

"Lauren, your mother is asking for you," Harry said.

"What's the matter?"

Harry cleared her throat.

Nicky stood up and placed her hand on Harry's arm in support.

Harry glanced at Nicky for a fraction of a second. "I'm sorry, Lauren, but she's not making sense. I think we are going to have to make our choices sooner rather than later."

"Damn, the fever probably has spiked. Have they called Doctor Green?" Lauren was on her feet ready to go. "I will go see her. First, Nicky, can you call your mother for me and then get those notes together?"

Without giving an answer, Nicky quickly dialed the number to connect to her mother. "Mom, Lori needs to speak with you."

Lauren took the phone and placed it against her ear. "Hi, Eden, I need to pick your brain, do you mind? ... Okay, here is the scenario. ..."

Nicky tugged on Harry's arm. "Yes."

"Want to take some air for a few minutes before things start to get even more hectic?"

Harry and Nicky turned away and went out the side door leaving Lauren talking with her mom.

∞

It was still early and the area was void of people as the two women sat on a bench close to a fountain. Soothed by the sounds of the trickling water, they sighed in unison

Harry put an arm around Nicky "When was the last time I told you I loved you?"

"Oh, ages and ages ago. All of an hour, I think." A soft chuckle accompanied the words.

"That long? Well, I must remember to tell you more often or you might think I'm neglecting you. I can't have that, can I?"

"Nope, you can't ... Harry?"

"Yeah?"

"How are you feeling about all this? I mean, how do you really feel and not what you want me to hear?"

Harry kissed the top of Nicky's head. "I'm bewildered, upset, angry, and scared for my mother, Lauren, and Steven."

"I can understand that but what about you? Aren't you all those things for yourself too?"

"Nicky, as long as you're here close to me I'll get by. You are my rock. With you beside me I can be their rock until it's all over one way or the other."

"You say it so matter-of-factly. She's your mother, Harry. You might lose more than a mother here. You know that don't you?"

"What do you mean?"

"Lauren."

"Lauren? Why will she be lost? Oh yeah, I know, it's hard to lose a parent."

Nicky moved and faced her lover before placing her hands around the face she adored even if Harry was dense about some things. "If something goes wrong with the drug, Harry, Lauren will probably go to prison."

A puzzled expression, which changed to astonishment, triggered in Harry's eyes. "She won't go alone."

Nicky tenderly reached up and kissed Harry's lips. "How about we go back and you tell Lauren just that."

"Tell her what?"

"That she's not alone in this and you're right with her every step of the way no matter where it takes you both."

"She knows that, Nicky. I'm here and arranging all the details, aren't I. If you want to be melodramatic I'm the accomplice or even the instigator."

As they walked back toward the building, Nicky smiled. "Yes, darling, but sometimes you need to say the words. Come on, no better time than now."

∞

Lauren's conversation with Eden Martin only increased her anxiety about administering the drug. The drug used in the jungle certainly wasn't as potent as what she would be using so the correct dosage was unknown. She had enough experience with experimental drugs to know how to go about this, but it was her mother and that, terrified her. There was no time for debate, she must do what she did best and administer the drug.

The visit to her mother confirmed what she thought. Victoria's fever was spiking and time was running out. She looked at her dad, walked a few steps to him, and gave him a hug. "How are you doing, Daddy?"

"Not too good, sweetheart. What about you?"

"Right now, I haven't a choice. I need to take care of my mother the best I can. Are you all right with this? I don't want to take the chance if you are not one hundred percent behind it."

"I don't see how we have any other choice, Lori. You, Harry, Nicky, your mother, and me are all in this together. We must go along with your mother's wishes. I don't see how we can deny her the one chance she has."

At that moment, a nurse entered the room and informed them that a state trooper was at the desk looking for them.

"It looks like the time has come, Lori. Shall we go see the trooper together?" He gently put his arm around her as they walked out to the nurse's station.

When they saw Harry and Nicky approaching, Steven quickly explained the situation.

Lauren glanced at her sister and wished she had Maggie at her side just as Nicky was at her sister's side. "Are you ready, Harry?"

"As I'll ever be. Lauren?"

"Yes?"

"Have you heard the expression 'all for one and one for all'?

Lauren shook her head and then realized what Harry was saying. She smiled and held out her hand.

Harry took the offered hand and they went to see the trooper.

After retrieving the medication, they all returned to Victoria's room.

Steven said, "If anyone has a doubt please state it now. We must be together in this."

Harry glanced down at Nicky. "We're in this for as long as you need us."

"Absolutely."

They all watched as Lauren prepared for the administration of the drug.

Lauren took the vial and filled a syringe with a small amount of the drug. Taking a deep breath, she injected it into the line. "God, if you're there, we need all the help we can get here." She looked at the others in the room. "Now it's a matter of wait and see. In about an hour, I will administer more of the drug."

"How long before we know?" Steven asked.

All eyes turned to Nicky; she was the only one likely to have any idea.

"We really have nothing to go by, Steven. The injections the boy my mother treated was the first generation of the drug. This one is the third generation. Although the medication is essentially the same structure, there were modifications that made it a much more powerful drug. To answer your question, I don't know."

"Thank you."

Lauren said, "I think we each need to take turns guarding the door from intruders. Do you all agree?"

"Yes," everyone said in unison.

"Leave that up to me, Lauren, I think I'm qualified for that task." Harry squeezed her sister's shoulder and started for the door.

"Harry, I will relieve you later, okay?" Steven said.

"Okay." Harry went out the door to keep her vigil outside the door.

"No one will get by Harry and she will feel like she's doing something useful. I know she hates waiting around."

"I have a feeling it will be a long night for us all, Nicky. Quite a partner you have there." Steven smiled broadly at Nicky.

∞

Harry stood outside Victoria's room and noticed a plaque on the wall across from her. *Funny, I usually don't miss things like that.* Taking a few steps, she read the poem as a tear trickled down her cheek.

We will smile once more
We call it a task
We call it adversary
We should call it a fear of the heart.
We can dodge the comment that hurts
We even see the pain that it causes
We see all that it is
We know what the cause is.
We shall see it through
We have family and friends that will do
We will cry that is sure

We will smile once more.

Chapter Twenty-four

Her heartbeat was practically nonexistent, her breathing shallow, and her body was in a state of lifelessness. Maggie's mind was deep in meditation as she readied herself for the journey back to Lauren. Such an undertaking, so soon after surgery, would be arduous at best. She would need all her coping skills if she were to succeed. Back to full consciousness, she slowly rose from the chair and made her way toward the door hanging onto the IV stand to steady herself.

"Exactly where to do you think you're going?"

"When did you get back?"

"That's unimportant. Where are you going?"

"You know where, Dad. Don't try to stop me."

"Why not give yourself another day or two to recover more?" It was more of an order than a question.

"No, Lauren needs me now. There is nothing you can do or say to stop me, Dad, so please stop trying."

"A lot of good you will do her if you can't stand on your own. Who will she be treating? Her mother or you?" Patrick moved toward his daughter.

"She is my strength. She is what I need to heal. I am what she needs to do what she must. Now, if you will excuse me, I have a helicopter to catch."

Patrick placed a gentle hand on her shoulder. "Please sit."

The perfect peace she attained was rapidly leaving her. "I told you, there's nothing you can do to stop me."

"I'm not trying to stop you, Megan, I just want to talk with you. Please, sit."

Her eyes pierced him. "That name is not to be used again and you know it. What are you trying to do? In case you forgot, I am Margaret now. Just say what you need to so I can go."

Patrick shook his head as a smile played around his mouth. "Of all my children you always were the most stubborn, Maggie. I knew this would be your response so I have arranged for Lydia to go with you."

"I don't need a nursemaid."

"In case you haven't noticed, you can barely get around. Just how do you plan to climb into the helicopter? You have the pack for your lung and the IV. How are you going to handle that all alone? Lydia will take care of those items for you. She will deposit you with Lauren then come back here. Do you have a better plan?"

Maggie blew out a breath as she began to sway before losing her balance.

Patrick broke her fall and helped her to stand again. "Please, sit."

Grateful for the chair, Maggie sat down unceremoniously—her injured arm and leg didn't allow her to fall gracefully. "As always, you are right, Dad. When can she be ready to go? I really need to be there. Lauren needs me. I can feel it."

Patrick picked up the house phone. "You can come in now with the wheelchair." He hung up the phone. "She will be right in and then you can be on your way. I imagine you might like to change out of that attractive gown into something a bit more suitable." He picked up a change of clothes from a nearby chair and offered them to her. "Will you do one thing for me?"

Maggie looked up at her father and reluctantly smiled. "Only one thing? That will be different." She took the clothes rested them on her lap.

Patrick laughed then bent down and gave her a kiss on the top of her head. "Yes, one thing. Please be careful."

"Lester is on life support and his cronies are all dead. I think it is safe now to be just me. Don't you?"

"Yes, it is safe now. But that's not what I mean. In your desire to be there for Lauren you may forget your own limitations and injure yourself further. Your mother would be very unhappy if that happens and she *will* blame me. So, please be careful."

"Sounds like you want me to cover your butt once more with Mom." Her smile broadened. "Yes, I will be careful." As her father stood up, she added, "Dad, thanks for caring."

"I will always care, Maggie. I love you."

"I love you too."

The door opened and a woman walked in the room pushing a wheelchair. "Ready to go?"

"Yep, let's get a move on I have a very important woman waiting for me." Maggie laughed. "First I need you to help me put these clothes on, Lydia."

"That would be a good idea." Lydia looked at Patrick who nodded before leaving the room. "Now, let's see if we can figure out the best way to do this."

Once dressed and in the chair Maggie heaved a sigh of relief. "That was harder than I thought it would be."

Lydia pushed the chair through the doors. "Keep that in mind. Your injuries are serious and the more movements you make the chance of undoing the repair will increase."

"I have no choice."

"You always have a choice, Margaret." Patrick said.

∞

Patrick watched as Lydia wheeled Maggie to the waiting helicopter. He held his breath as the pilot and nurse helped his daughter into the craft letting it out when he saw her strapped into the seat. Once the helicopter was airborne, he picked up the phone.

"She is on her way. How soon can you be in place? … Good. See to it that her room is ready and it is in the ICU unit. … The rotation will be round the clock … No harm will come to any of them … Good we agree."

∞

Harry stood in front of Victoria's ICU room. No one was getting by her. A nurse approached the room. "You can't go in there."

"Excuse me? This is my patient and I will see to it that the rule of one visitor at a time is enforced. Now get out of my way."

Harry looked at the nametag and gave the woman a once over. "Nurse Hatchet, I don't think you understand."

"Hatcher, the name is Hatcher."

"Whatever. They are having a prayer meeting and I am sure you don't want to interrupt. Now you run along and when they're done I will come and get you."

"Just who do you think you are? Get out of my way or I will call security."

Harry moved between the woman and the door. "No, I don't think you will."

"Do you think I am going to be intimidated by the likes of you? I said, get out of my way."

Just at that moment, Doctor Green arrived. "Please, Nurse, keep your voice down. Is there a problem here?"

"I should say there is. This woman won't let me in my patient's room. They are obviously violating hospital rules by having three visitors at once. I am the supervisor for this wing and I insist that the rules be followed."

"Nurse Hatchet."

"Hatcher, the name is Hatcher."

"Whatever. You are not to go into that room again for any reason. Do I make myself clear? I will not allow my patient or her family upset by you. As far as you're concerned, the rules do not apply to them. Do I make myself clear?"

"But ..."

"Do I make myself clear, Hatchet?"

"Hatcher. Fine, I will have to see what the hospital administrator has to say about this. Doctor Goldstein will not be happy with you, Doctor Green."

"Go ahead but you should know in advance he will agree with me."

"We'll see about that."

Harry listened to the exchange and noted a sense of fear in the doctor's voice. The name Resnik came to mind and with certainty, she knew he was involved with the doctor and the hospital. *Can one man have that much power?*

The door opened and Lauren emerged. "What is going on out here?"

Harry looked at her sister and smiled. "Some nurse thought she could order me around." She chuckled and winked at Lauren. "Imagine that."

Lauren smiled. "I can only imagine. Why don't you go on in, Harry? Mom is asking for you."

"Doctor Walker, may I have a word in private." Doctor Green took Lauren by the arm, led her into a small office, and closed the door.

∞

"Have you gotten test results back? Is it bad news?"

"No, not at all. I want you to know that if this were my mother I would be doing the same thing. If you need someone to consult with or to give you a break, I will be honored to help."

Lauren looked thoughtfully at the man. "Doctor Green, thank you. I can't begin to tell you what that means to me. But, I can't let you risk everything. The fewer people involved the better. If you could just make sure I can get tests run, I would appreciate that."

"How many doses have you given her?"

"I will give the second one in about thirty minutes."

"Any improvement?"

"Not really, but she has stopped her slide downwards so I'm taking that as a positive." She smiled fondly at the man. "Thank you again."

"You're welcome. Do you want another nurse? I promise she will be discreet." He smiled. "I'm not sure I'd be as brave as you are by risking everything … then again given the chance if my mom was as sick as yours, I would hope I'd have the same courage and love."

Lauren nodded. "Thank you and no, like I said, the fewer involved the better. I need to get back now.

"Good luck," he whispered.

She turned, opened the door, and was gone.

Lauren felt the hairs on her neck prickle as she left the room. Then a sense of warmth overtook her as she looked around the hallway. Eyes filled with love focused on her. She quickly crossed the space then couched down. "Maggie, you're here." Tears of joy filled Laruen's eyes as she laid her head in Maggie's lap.

∞

The first thing she noticed was that the hand resting on her head was cold. When she raised her head, she noticed, for the first time, the bruises and the dark circles under Maggie's eyes. Taking the hand into hers, she gently felt for the pulse. It was rapid—not a good sign.

"Maggie, look at you. You should be in a bed." As she looked her over, she was horrified at what she saw. "How did you get here?"

Maggie raised her hand and point. "Lydia."

"Lydia, I'm Lauren Walker, Maggie's doctor. Why on earth did anyone let her travel in this condition?"

Maggie grabbed her hand and shook her head. "Me, I did it, not Lydia."

"Apparently, Doctor, she insisted and gave her father no choice but to let her go. I came along to make sure she arrived here safely. I have the orders for her medications and all the charts and x-rays for you. I believe there is an ICU bed for her." She handed Lauren the portfolio of information.

"Thank you, Lydia. I'm sorry I was upset with you. I do know how stubborn she can be. I appreciate all you've done." She shook the women's hand. "Have a safe journey and will you please tell Patrick that I will make sure she recovers fully."

"Certainly." Lydia smiled before turning and walking away.

"Now you, Ms. Sullivan, will listen to me and do exactly as I say. You stay put and I will be right back after I speak with Dr. Green." Lauren pointed to a man standing at the nurse's station.

All Maggie could manage was a small smile.

Lauren returned and knelt by the wheelchair. "Your room is ready and Doctor Green will be your physician." She shook her head. "I don't know whether to be angry or overjoyed with you. Do you know the chance you took, Maggie? What would I do if I lost you? Please, don't do this again."

Maggie's breathing labored. "I love you."

Lauren stood up and gently hugged Maggie. "That's always a safe card to play and I love you too." She kissed the bruised cheek, went to the back of the wheelchair, and began pushing it. "What do you say we get you settled and then you can sleep?"

∞

Harry slowly entered the hospital room and glanced around. It hadn't changed much since she was last there an hour ago.

"Harriet?"

Harry heard the feeble voice as she walked toward the bed. Victoria's eyes immediately captured her. "Victoria, how are you feeling?"

Steven and Nicky moved away to give them a degree of privacy.

Harry bent down to hear the words. "All the better for seeing you. Where's Lauren?"

"She'll be here soon." She knew that might be a slight exaggeration as she'd seen Maggie enter the corridor and she didn't look much better than Victoria.

"I wanted to say thank you, Harriet."

"For what?" Harry sat carefully on the side of the bed and dipped her head as close as she could to hear her mother's voice.

"For being here with me. Lauren will need you."

"Hey, Lauren has Maggie and doesn't need a big sister."

"Yes, she has Maggie but blood is thicker than water. I know she needs you in her life, especially now."

Harry wanted to shrug off the seemingly easy way the woman gave her family responsibilities. She hadn't convinced herself it was right, however, she wasn't about to argue the point. One thing was certain—Victoria was very near death. "Oh, when you are up and about again, I think she will see me as one big deterrent to her plans."

"Plans?"

Ooops. Did I leave the cat out of the bag? "Well, not plans exactly. At least no more than most couples make along the way."

Harry watched as Victoria's face took on a concentrated look as if she were puzzling out something she didn't quite grasp. She beckoned Nicky forward. "You asked me yesterday if I had anyone important in my life and, I told you I was a loner. Remember?"

"Yes, I feel sorry for you, Harriet. You need someone in your life that you can turn to for all life's wonders and trials." Victoria's eyes blinked constantly.

"I do though. This is Nicky and she *is* that part of my life."

A slurred sound, which could have been Nicky's name, came from the woman in the bed.

"She's more than that. She's the love of my life. With her I know I'll never be alone."

Victoria tried to smile before her eyes closed once again.

∞

"Where did she go, Harry?" Nicky asked. They left the room so Steven could have a little private time with his wife. They had expected to see Lauren outside the room but she wasn't anywhere around.

"She was here when I came back. Ah, yes. Maggie turned up."

"Maggie? Are you sure?"

"Yeah. I'd remember that woman from a great distance but she looks like crap." Harry swiveled her head and saw good old nurse 'Hatchet'

"Nurse Hatchet, have you seen, Doctor Walker?"

"Hatcher, the name is Hatcher. Got it?"

Harry's eyebrow raised a fraction and she was just about to retaliate with a similar sharp response when Nicky interceded.

"Sorry, Nurse Hatcher, my friend here is a little short sighted. She left her glasses at home. I wonder if you could help us please. Doctor Walker was here a little while ago and she seems to have disappeared."

"Seems your buddy Walker found herself another patient."

"Yes. She's another friend of ours. It really isn't our day, is it? Can you tell us where they went please?"

Harry glared at Nicky.

"I think they went to the room at the end of the corridor."

"Oh, you are wonderful, Nurse Hatcher, thanks. Would you mind if we dropped by to make sure everything is okay? I know it's against the rules to have so many people in the room but she's a good friend and we'll only be a few minutes?"

"That won't be a problem, dear. Please be sure you leave quickly.

Harry had to give it to Nicky; she sure could pour the syrup on the sour apple. She saw the nurse smile briefly at her lover and then give her a cold unfriendly glance. "I can't believe you sucked up to her, Nicky. She would have done as she was told." Harry shook her head at Nicky as they proceeded to the room.

"Yeah and we would have one more problem on our plates if she ever finds out what is going on. Now, she might just ignore us. Come on, we need Lauren." Nicky walked away leaving her partner standing silently with a goofy grin on her face.

As they looked into the room, they saw a very ill looking Maggie hooked up to monitors. Lauren was holding her hand with her head resting on the bed.

"I don't think we should disturb them, Nicky."

The statement was irrelevant.

Nicky walked over to Lauren. "Hey, sleepyhead, you're needed in your Mother's room."

Lauren looked around. "What's up? Has she taken a turn for the worse?"

Harry noticed her sister's pale cheeks that accentuated her weary state. Lauren was nothing like the woman she met for the first time a week or so ago.

"No. It's time for the next dose."

"Oh, right. Okay, let's go then." She kissed Maggie. "Nicky, she isn't doing well at all. Do you think you could sit with her until I get back?"

"Want me to stay and Nicky go with you for support?"

Two pairs of startled eyes stared at Harry.

Nicky shook her head and looked at Harry with amazement. "Of course I will, Lori. You two go ahead and I'll stay here with Maggie." She squeezed her friend's arm and winked at her lover. "Take all the time you need. I won't let anything happen to her, Lori."

∞

Nicky looked at the broken body of her friend's lover. Over the years in the jungle, she had seen her share of damaged bodies but nothing like what was before her. Bruises covered both her arms along with numerous cuts. Many stitched but most healing on their own. "What happened to you, Maggie? What secrets are you keeping from my friend?"

"She has no secrets from Lauren."

Nicky turned and saw an unfamiliar woman standing in the doorway and moved between her and Maggie. "Who are you and how would you know whether they have secrets or not?"

"Oh, I know and you will have to trust me on that one."

The woman's voice and manner held no hint of deception or danger.

"Just who exactly are you that you think I should trust you without question? Are you a doctor or something?"

"No, the name is Carolyn Connelly. I am a relative of Meg ... I mean Maggie."

"Do you know Maggie's father? If you're a relative you will know why I ask that."

"Oh, yes. I know Patrick and I understand that he will hunt anyone down who harms a hair on her head. How is she doing?"

"I'm not really sure as I just got here myself. From the looks of her, I would say she was in some hell of a fight." For some reason, Nicky found it easy to trust this woman.

"Yes, she was. Do you mind if I sit with you? I would like to be here when she wakes up." She walked further into the room and sat in the chair by the bed.

Nicky fixed the woman with a gaze. "No, I don't mind. Do you think she will?"

"I am certain she will not."

"Then, I will leave you here with her and find my friends. I know she will be in good hands."

∞

"Was she coherent when you saw her, Harry?"

"Yes. She was very lucid. Fell asleep shortly afterwards but it was a restful sleep."

"How do you feel about all this, Harry?" Lauren was desperate to know how her older sister felt since she gave so little away. There was however, the odd crack did appear in the solid wall Harry erected.

"Feel?" Harry looked at her. "Bewildered I guess. If that makes any sense?"

"Yes it makes sense. It's about the only thing that does. I feel as if my world has shattered into tiny splinters and keeps pricking at every conscious thought and action. I know they prepared us in medical school for the worst but I don't think this was in the handbook. God, knows, I wouldn't want it to happen to my worst enemy. Well, maybe one of Maggie's."

"I'd feel the same way if Nicky turned up in the state Maggie has. Maybe one day you might want to talk about it?"

Lauren glanced up and saw compassion shining brightly out of those often ice cold eyes. "I'd like that when this is all over."

"You have a date." Harry's smiled and winked at her.

"Let's go help mom."

They entered the room and Steven stood up in relief.

∞

Lauren selected another vial from the lockable container in the small fridge in the room and measured out the dosage required. Her mother had stabilized as far as she could tell and Doctor Green had confirmed the initial findings. He had been cautiously optimistic about the situation and allowed a smile to tug at his lips. He'd even taken the opportunity to take Steven for a break and discuss his wife's condition.

Her father had gone because he felt better discussing this aspect than waiting around. He was grateful for the doctor's time.

Lauren sucked in a deep breath and went to the bed. Before she inserted the needle into the drip line, she waited and stared at her mother. For all of her life she had been so vital and completely in control of everything around her. Or so it appeared. How appearances could be deceptive. For years, a man blackmailed her mother and they hadn't had a clue. Victoria was domineering; however, that was just one of her characteristics. She had always loved her family, some had said almost to the point of claustrophobia. She and her father had never seen it that way because they knew the truth. They had allowed her to think she was dictating things when they could actually talk her around with a reasonable argument—she was a lawyer after all.

"Lori, are you okay?" Harry asked. "Have you changed your mind?

Startled at the question, Lauren blinked a couple of times. "No. Why do you ask?"

Harry gave her a crooked smile and Lauren saw her eyes travel to the syringe poised over the line.

The door to the room opened.

Nicky, with a gentle expression on her face walked in. "Hi, is everything okay?"

"What are you doing here?" Lauren shouted.

Nicky's eyes opened wide. "Why, I came to see if everything was …"

"I asked you to stay with Maggie until I came back. Why are you here?" Tears welled in Lauren's eyes.

Harry stepped between Lauren and her lover. "Nicky, is Maggie okay?"

Nicky blinked back a tear of her own. "Yes, I left her in good hands."

Harry placed a finger under Nicky's chin. "Whose?"

"She said her name was Caroline Connelly. She's okay. She's a relative."

Lauren, with the drug still in the syringe, walked for the door.

"Where do you think you're going?"

"Maggie might be in danger. How can Nicky know if this person is really a relative? I need to see her now." Lauren's eyes darted around trying to find another exit as Harry continued to block her way.

Nicky sucked in a deep breath.

"What about our mother?"

"Maggie needs me. She doesn't have anyone else that she can rely on to help her." She scowled at Nicky. "I'm the only one she can depend on."

"Want to give me the drug and I'll give Victoria her next dose?"

Lauren looked at the syringe and closed her eyes at the realization at how totally bent out of shape she was. Her emotions were getting the better of her and she needed to concentrate or she could lose both her mother and Maggie. "I… Oh, God, I'm sorry, Harry." She crumbled into her sister's strong hold.

"Hey, that's okay. Come on now, it's a hard time for us all but especially you. I'll go and be with Maggie until you come by and take over. I promise not to leave her, even if her father comes by. What do you think of that?"

Tearful eyes looked up into Harry's and Lauren gave her sister a watery smile. "You promise?"

"Absolutely. Nicky will stay with you until you come for me and then I'll come back here and wait with Nicky and your dad."

Lauren went back toward the bed and her task.

Harry smiled briefly and left the room.

Chapter Twenty-five

Maggie had seen a wonderful scene in her dreamscape, although anything that held Lauren in it would be magnificent. It reminded her of the first time they met; a beautiful natural surrounding with a river flowing gracefully by them as they enjoyed a marvelous feast laid out on a plaid blanket. The wonderful thing about this dream was they were as close as one could be. They were completely naked and supremely happy. If she opened her eyes would the dream disappear leaving her wanting her lover as she had the moment conscious thought allowed her any feelings at all.

As she had always and would always do, she suspected, until her dying day, she dared fate by opening her eyes. A face so very familiar to her swam in front of her. No, she knew she was definitely dreaming because what she saw couldn't be.

"Hey, Meg, darling, are you coming around to see me?" Caroline whispered.

Maggie's eyes fluttered open, closed, and then opened again. "Is it really you?"

"Here, drink this, Meg, it will help."

Maggie felt a straw and sucked on it craving the moisture it gave her parched mouth. It stung the back of her throat but it felt marvelous. Her eyes tried to focus clearly on the woman holding her head tenderly.

"Baby, that's enough for now. Let me fluff up those pillows for you. As always, you manage to make a mess of your bedclothes."

"Mom, I've missed you." Maggie's tears dripped unceremoniously down her cheeks.

The woman stopped her pillow arranging and held her child close. "I've missed you too, Meg. Why didn't you want to come home to us?"

"You know I couldn't, Mom. I've missed you all so very much. It broke my heart sometimes to see you all as a family and know I couldn't be with you."

"What? What do you mean, Meg? When?" She rocked Maggie tenderly.

A tearful smile greeted the quick fire questions. "Christmas carol singing at church, your birthday, yours and dad's anniversary, it was the big four-o wasn't it? Christie's christening and Randal's twenty-first, to name but a few."

"Oh, darling, why didn't you let us know you were there? Did your father know?"

"No. No, Mom. He would have hauled me before you all with my new face and name and proudly announced me to the world again." Maggie was feeling better. It was like an elixir of life to have someone love and cherish her as her mother did.

"Why didn't you come home, Meg? Your dad would have protected us."

Maggie contemplated the lost years with her family. "He would have tried but they would have found me with you. I know it. I didn't like being alone, Mom. I hated it. I love you all so much. I felt like it was the end of the world when I was by myself and there was no one else I could turn to. Dad did his best to visit but that wasn't very often. There were times when I felt so lonely I wanted to end it all."

Caroline sucked in a breath then exhaled slowly. "You are stronger than that, darling. You always have been. After all, you are your father's daughter."

"I am, aren't I? He wouldn't ever give up, would he? He'd find a solution to any problem. Can you ever find a solution to thinking that love has passed you by, Mom?"

"Are you talking about family, darling?"

Maggie looked at her mother as she leaned back on the fluffed up pillows. "I love you all, Mom. I was so sad. It was like you were wrenched away from me for no reason, I hadn't done anything wrong."

"Oh, Meg, don't be so hard on yourself. You are here now and no way are you not going to be part of the family again. In fact, your brother announced he's getting married in six months. This time I won't allow you to hide in the shadows."

"Oh, Mom, I've missed you so much." Tears of joy sprang from Maggie's eyes as they did her mother's.

∞

Harry entered the room the door barely making a noise as it opened. The tender scene unfolding in front of her gave her pause. From the lack of reaction by the two women in the room, it was obvious that they didn't hear or notice her enter the room. She decided to eavesdrop on the conversation. Lauren would expect no less. Nicky, on the other hand, would probably be upset.

Harry was stock still as she watched the exchange. Here were all the elements that happened to her, in a different way of course, though similar, nonetheless. Maybe now she knew why she hadn't liked Maggie from the start. They had a familiar experience, albeit of differing magnitude. She had been the luckier of the two of them. Here was Maggie, who had given up her family for whatever reason. She, on the other hand, had never known her immediate family, but had always missed them, craved them, knowing deep down that they were out there some place but she wasn't allowed inside. It hurt. It hurt like hell.

"Your dad tells me you've found a really nice girl and you've decided to settle down with. Was it that lovely girl in here with you earlier?"

"Lauren, yeah, it was probably Lauren. Oh, Mom, you are going to love her I know it. She's kind, caring, beautiful, fantastic, and loves me and gives me a hard time. It's everything wonderful in life."

The older woman, Maggie's mother, would be a surprise when she met Lauren. The realization that Maggie's mother had only seen Nicky was a double-edged sword. She was proud that this woman thought Nicky was all those things but an irrational jealous element reared its head as Maggie talked

Maggie's mother laughed. "Well, she needs to have all those wonderful characteristics, as well as others, to put up with you."

Harry decided that it was time to leave for it was not her reunion. What she had heard though, gave her something to think about regarding her feelings for her mother.

Exiting the room, she literally bumped into Lauren.

"Hey, I was …"

"You promised me you wouldn't leave until I came."

Lauren's glare was enough to singe her eyebrows. "Extenuating circumstances, sis. Go inside and you will find out what I mean." Harry held back the curtain and Lauren passed her with an irritated look.

"I will."

∞

Lauren stood in the doorway and saw a blonde woman sitting on Maggie's bed holding her hand. Maggie was uncharacteristically crying, her face flushed and yet pale. It didn't appear that Maggie was in any danger but still, she felt something must be amiss.

"Is everything okay in here?" She walked quickly over to the opposite side of the bed. Her hand automatically reached to feel Maggie's forehead before she took her wrist to check the pulse. All the while, she was discreetly looking at the woman opposite her. The only way to describe the stranger was she looked like everyone's mother should look. She had a warm, friendly face and although slightly overweight, you could not call her fat.

Maggie looked at Lauren for a long time. "Everything is wonderful, Lauren." A dazzling smile crossed her face as she took Lauren's hand in hers. "I want you to meet my mother, Caroline Connelly." Then turning to her mother, she said. "Mom, this is the woman I love, Lauren Walker."

Caroline beamed as she stretched her hand out to Lauren. "It's wonderful to meet you at last, Doctor Walker. I have heard so much about you. It's as if I already know you."

Lauren stood with her mouth opened. She saw the offered hand but couldn't move to shake it. Maggie's coughing finally got her attention. She took the hand and shook it vigorously. "Mrs. Connelly, it's a pleasure to meet you. It's nice to know you have heard so much about me as I have heard absolutely nothing about you."

Caroline pulled her hand away and gave Lauren her best motherly smile. "Well then, I would say it was about time we got to know each other better. Wouldn't you?" She patted her daughter's shoulder. "Meg, your description of Lauren didn't do her justice. She is even lovelier."

Lauren looked at Maggie and frowned.

"What's the matter, Lauren? I only told Mom the truth about you. You are kind, caring, beautiful, fantastic, and love me. Why are you frowning like that? Is something the matter?" Maggie eyebrows knitted. "Is it your mother?"

"No. My mother has stabilized for the moment. I need to go now. It was lovely meeting you, Mrs. Connelly." With that, she turned to leave the room.

"Wait. Please, Lauren, don't go. Not like this."

"Mom, will you please give us a few minutes alone?"

"Certainly, sweetie." She kissed her daughter on the cheek before leaving the room. As she passed Lauren she whispered, "Thank you for taking care of her."

Maggie held her hand out for Lauren. "Please, come here."

Lauren reluctantly walked to the bed and took the offered hand. She couldn't stop the tears welling up in her eyes from falling.

"Lauren, what's the matter? Please tell me so I can make it right."

The day had been long. Lauren's body was feeling the results of the emotional roller coaster from not only her mother but Maggie as well. *How much more can I endure?* "Meg, is that short for Megan? Is that your real name? You trusted me so little you couldn't share that with me?" Even as she said the words, she knew how petty and ridiculous she sounded. "What other surprises do you have in store for me, Maggie, or should I say, Meg?"

Maggie pulled Lauren close and kissed her. "I told you I had another name and it would be dangerous for you to know. When I met you, Maggie came to life full force and the other person I was disappeared. Meg is gone. I am still me. What's that saying about a rose by any other name smelling as sweet? I love you with every fiber of my being, Lauren Walker. A different name will never change that."

The long hours and exhaustion finally overtook Lauren and she cried. "Maggie, I am so sorry. I love you so much. Please forgive me."

Maggie patted the bed and Lauren obliged by crawling next to her. Carefully placing her arm around Lauren, she drifted off into the first restful sleep of the day.

∞

Harry was asleep in the chair as Steven gently nudged Nicky. Her attention grew away from her observation of Victoria to her lover.

"She hasn't had any sleep for over twenty-four hours. I guess it's finally taking its toll on her body."

Nicky watched the quiet rise and fall of Harry's chest. She looked vulnerable in sleep. It had always fascinated her when, on rare occasions, she had awoken before Harry and simply watched her sleep.

"Why don't you take her back to the hotel and get a couple of hours rest? We'll call if there is any significant change. It looks like Vicky is sleeping peacefully."

"Do you mind? I hate to leave you and I'm not sure Harry will want to go." Nicky was still stinging from when Lauren verbally attacked her after leaving Maggie alone with a stranger.

"If you ask her, she'll go." Steven winked at her and motioned for her to do just that.

"Thanks, Steven. Will you explain to Lauren please? I would hate for her to think we abandoned you."

Steven smiled. "Leave the explanation to me. Lauren will understand."

"Thanks."

∞

Half an hour later, they were in the hotel room. Harry was exhausted and although she had protested that she couldn't leave, it hadn't taken much persuasion to have her come back to the hotel.

"Why not have a shower, Harry, and get some rest."

Harry stared bleary eyed at Nicky and gave her a wry smile, "Am I that bad?"

Nicky wrinkled her nose. "No. Go have a shower and get into bed. I guarantee that as soon as your head hits the pillow you'll be asleep."

"You think so, do you? What if I said I'd rather do something more than sleep in bed? Care to join me?"

Nicky flashed Harry a grin and placed a loving kiss at the side of her mouth, "Go shower."

As Nicky thought, Harry fell asleep as soon as she lay on the bed. Except for the small nocturnal sounds that occasionally emanated from the bed the room was silent. She decided to indulge in a long bath to soak away the strain of the past few hours while waiting for Harry to wake up. The conversation she had with her mother and the notes she read were uppermost on her mind as she poured a complimentary bubble bath into the water.

Two hours later, Nicky, curled up on the bed, felt fingers tracing her abdomen. She knew the touch and her body's response was immediate and electric.

"You're awake?"

"Yeah, I feel refreshed and ready for anything."

Nicky angled her body, which had her side-by-side with Harry so they faced each other. "Anything, huh?"

"Oh, yes. Do you have anything in mind?"

The same sexy grin that she had fallen for in the conference room more than a year earlier when she first met Harry was on her face. "I can think of lots of wonderful things but maybe we should think about going back to the hospital?"

"Steven told you he would call if there was a change, didn't he?"

"Yes. Although, I thought maybe you would want to be close by." Nicky was surprised at the relaxed stance of her partner and it made her smile.

"I am close by and there isn't much I can do at the moment."

"How do you feel about your mother now, Harry?"

"I ache inside, Nicky. I still don't understand why she left me like she did."

Nicky saw the doubt and the war that Harry was waging with age old fears of loneliness and the need to belong to a family that loved and wanted her. Nicky relaxed into Harry's chest and sighed softly as she responded to the uncertainty in her lover. "It's all about letting go, Harry."

"Yes, I know. You don't understand, Nicky. I thought I had and it was all behind me."

"What changed your mind?"

"It reminded me of the pain, hurt and resentfulness I felt. I'm not sure I want to go there again"

Puzzled, Nicky guessed there was more to this conversation than Victoria, "Resentfulness?"

"Yes. I resented Abby leaving me alone. It hurt so much that I don't want to go through that again and I won't."

"Do you still feel like that now?" Nicky's own insecurity rose up to greet her once more. It was hard enough to live up to a dead lover, but one that was your sister, who you loved as well, was nearly impossible.

"No. I did let Abby go, Nicky. I could never have loved you as I do if I hadn't. This is about possibly watching someone that you have only just allowed into your heart die. How can I do that if I know what the outcome is?"

Nicky had known that, how could she think otherwise. Harry was a one love person. Their time together may not be in years but the love they shared felt like it. Everything they did together was as if they had experienced it a thousand times before. "I thought you were great with your mother."

"You know me, Nic. I can learn the rules of engagement fast."

"You say it as if it's a boardroom battle strategy."

"Nic, it is. This way I don't get hurt. I can be charming, helpful and eventually I'll understand what's needed and deal with it."

To Nicky, Harry's voice sounded like she had found the only possible solution to her problems of handling the mother-daughter routine. She smiled and turned so she rested on her side right next to Harry. The feeling of closeness was overpowering her senses and all she wanted to do now was kiss Harry to distraction. But, the issue was too important to let it take second place to the passion that was building inside her. She saw Harry's eyes glaze and she knew that her arousal wasn't one-sided. "All that's needed, darling, is your love."

"You have all my love, Nicky."

Nicky captured the lips that had spoken those tender loving feelings and her heart fluttered incessantly as their passion rose. It was hard to pull away but she knew she had to. "I don't mind sharing a tiny piece of your love if it remains in the family."

"Did I tell you that it was Maggie's mother that you left in the room with her?"

Nicky's passion extinguished suddenly as her interest sparked. "Maggie's mother? Tell me more, Harry."

Harry chuckled and proceeded to tell her what she heard. "The upside is that for some reason Maggie hasn't seen her family for a while but it looked like everything is going to be okay from now on. She missed her family."

"Oh, that sounds so mysterious and tragic. I'm glad she can finally become part of them again. She must have been so lonely. Poor Maggie."

"Yeah, poor Maggie. Nic?"

"Hmmm, what is it?"

"I don't want to go through that and feel lonely all over again."

Nicky gave her lover a long serious gaze and stroked her cheek with a feather light touch. "I love you, Harry, and you know that. Right?"

"Yes. I know it and you know I love you too. Right?"

"I know it. Your love is like every breath I take. Do you know what I found out a long time ago, Harry, about loving and leaving?"

Ice blue eyes focused on her. "What."

"If we are lucky, we will love many people in our lives for all different reasons. Family, friends, and lovers. Some stay a lifetime; others fall by the wayside and some we simply have to let go though we don't want to. All I know for sure is that no matter how long we love someone it will always hurt when they leave no matter what the reason. However, we will always be the richer for sharing that love with them. It is the experience of life and if we don't allow it in, our lives can be barren."

"Are you saying my life is barren because I won't let my mother inside?"

"Not you, Harry. How could it be? You loved Abby and you love me. All I want you to know is that no matter the potential hurt, you don't let that blind you to how wonderful loving someone can be in the giving and receiving of that love."

"I can try, Nicky."

"I know you will, and that's all anyone can ask."

"Is there anything else I need to know?" Harry waited and Nicky kissed her lips then began to placing small kisses all over Harry's face and neck before moving to her chest.

Harry responded with equal passion.

∞

Lauren smiled when she felt fingers gently stroking her cheek. That action made her know that Maggie was keeping her safe. "Hmmm, never leave me."

"I am yours for all time. Good morning beautiful."

Lauren's body filled with happiness as her mind slowly woke. "Morning? Oh, my God, my mother. I didn't give her the next dose of medicine."

Maggie struggled with the IV lines trying to reach out to Lauren. "Lauren, it's okay. Doctor Green did it."

"No, he can't, it isn't right." All she needed was one more person risking their license on this. It was bad enough her sister put her job on the line but now Doctor Green did too. "Damn, why didn't I wake up? Shit. I need to go see how she is doing."

Maggie grabbed Lauren's wrist. "Wait a minute. Take a deep breath and wake up first. You won't do her any good like this."

Lauren sucked in a breath. "You're right. I just can't believe I slept through it. Why didn't anyone come and get me?" Then she noticed the pained look on Maggie's face. "Hey, are you okay? How do you feel?" Her hand automatically felt Maggie's forehead for a fever.

"I'm fine." Maggie took Lauren's hand in hers and kissed it gently.

"Looks like the two of you finally woke up," Caroline Connelly said.

"Mom, you came back."

"Of course I did, silly. Where did you think I would go when my little girl needs me?" A big motherly smile was on her face.

Lauren got off the bed and walked over to the pleasant woman. "Mrs. Connelly, it is so good to see you. I'm sorry for the way I acted last night."

"Not a problem at all, dear. I will be here with Meg if you want to go and see your mom."

"Thank you very much. I do need to see how she is doing. Maggie, I will be back shortly. Don't go anywhere without me,"

∞

Lauren entered her mother's room and saw her father with his head resting on his arms as he bent over on the bed. She shook him gently. "Dad, wake up."

"Huh. What? Is she okay?"

"Everything is fine. Why don't you go back to the hotel and get some sleep. I will stay here with mom.

Steven stretched as he stood up. "Darling, I can't leave her. What if she needs me? What if …"

"Dad, you won't do her any good if you're exhausted. Go sleep and I will be here. Harry should be back soon and I will call you if anything happens, promise." She was leading him to the door. "There is no debate here, Dad. Go, get some sleep and I will take care of mom."

"But …"

"No. I said *no*. Go and rest and I will call you. Now go." She rose on her toes and kissed his cheek. "Please, Dad."

"You will call, right?"

"Yes. Now go, please." Lauren was glad when her father relented and headed out the door. She turned back to her mother and glanced at her watch. It was time for another dose. *I wonder how long before we see results?*

After drawing the proper amount, she injected the medicine into the IV line. She sat down and once again read the notes Nicky's mother had sent. She wasn't sure how much time had passed when she felt a hand touch hers. She looked at her mother and saw eyes focused on her.

"Hey, welcome back." She stood up and read the monitors. "How are you feeling?"

Victoria attempted to speak and pointed to the water pitcher by the bed.

"Just a small sip, Mom," Lauren held the cup for her mother while she sipped water through the straw. "There you go. Is that better?"

A smile came to Victoria's face as she began to become more cognizant. "Thank you. What happened?"

A puzzled look came over Lauren's face. "You don't remember?"

Victoria nodded. "Yes. Infection, dying, and a new drug … it's kind of fuzzy."

"That's right. It looks like the drug is working." She instinctively touched her mother's forehead. "You're much cooler now."

Victoria closed her eyes. "I'm tired." She fell into a light sleep.

Lauren smiled and added to her notes about the latest dosage and her mother's response. When she heard voices, she looked up to see her sister and Nicky entering the room.

"Hi, good news, she was awake for a little while."

"That's wonderful news, Lauren. When did she wake?" Harry asked.

"Just a little while ago. She remembered all that has happened. Well sort of anyway." Lauren was finally beginning to be cautiously optimistic about her mother's condition.

"Sort of?"

Lauren smiled at her sister's apparent attempt to cover her concern. "She didn't remember all the details but she knew what had happened and why."

"Oh. What does that mean?" Harry asked.

Lauren turned to her sister and Nicky and smiled. "It looks like the drug is working, but I still have some questions about the dosage and the length of treatment. Do you think we can call your parents and get their thoughts?"

Nicky grinned. "Yeah, my mom will be itching to hear how things have gone. I know I would. A chip off the old block, you know."

Harry turned to Nicky. "Yep, I'll guarantee she's a chip off the old block, Lauren. Be careful, or they might be dissecting every minute detail." A rich chuckle followed the comment.

"Thank you. I will heed your warning, Harry."

Lauren couldn't help but smile.

"That's great. This means I need to have the tests done as soon as possible."

"Tests? What tests are you talking about, Harry? I think Mom's advances are all the tests we need at the moment."

"Have you forgotten that she still requires a kidney and that I'm looking like the only candidate?"

Lauren looked at her sister for a moment. "Harry, are you sure? It isn't a small procedure and is not without its risks."

A serious, thoughtful expression crossed Harry's face as she turned to Lauren. "Didn't I say I was here until the end? When I mean the end, I mean there is no going back until we resolve the situation."

"Harry, I don't know what to say. Will thank you be enough?"

"Yes, that will do nicely. Anyway, you're not the only one who can take a risk or two in this family. Right?" Harry winked at her then turned to Nicky.

"You two ladies go talk with Eden and I'll stand guard over Vic … Mother. You never know, good old nurse Hatchet might decide to poke her nose around the door."

"Thank you, Harry. I would appreciate that very much. She should sleep for a bit longer I think." A brilliant smile crossed Lauren's face.

"How about you get yourself a decent meal. Nicky could do with breakfast too and I'll have a bagel and coffee when you come back." Harry moved toward the chair by the bed placing a hand on Lauren's shoulder.

Weariness began to settle into Lauren's being. "Thank you, Harry."

"Nic, maybe you two should have breakfast before you talk with your mom," Harry said. "Don't skip breakfast little, sis, you need the energy."

A smile played around Nicky's mouth. "I'll do that. Do you want anything inside the bagel?"

"Well, how about a scrambled egg." Harry grinned and settled down in the chair next to the bed.

∞

The door close silently behind Nicky and Lauren and Harry turned back to her vigil. *It's strange how I now think of Victoria as my mother.* It was funny how a situation could totally change one's outlook. *Although, to be truthful I still haven't forgiven her for abandoning me as a baby.*

Harry sat bedside gazing at the profile of her mother, wondering if she had any of her facial resemblance at all—she didn't think so. Maybe they had character traits alike. She would have to explore that eventually if she was given the time.

Victoria began to mumble in her sleep. All of it was incoherent except for a word or two. One word caught her attention. *Grandchild.*

Grandchild? Who has children? She didn't think that Lauren had any and she certainly hadn't any. Harry listened intently waiting to see if Victoria would say anymore.

Victoria opened her eyes and looked around the room. When she saw Harry, tears began to flow. "You came. Oh, I am so sorry. I tried to protect you. I am sorry."

Harry leaned forward and placed a hand on Victoria's in an attempt to soothe her. "What did you mean that you tried to protect me?"

"The mayor—didn't know he was so evil—he killed them. I am so sorry. Please forgive me."

"Hush, Victoria, hush, everything is okay now. He's dead and can't hurt you now."

"You don't understand," Victoria cried.

Harry gave her mother a wide-eyed look. "I do understand, I promise. Why don't you tell me what's troubling you? We will work it out. They tell me I'm good at working stuff out."

"He killed my grandchild. I am so sorry, Harriet, I had no idea."

Stunned by the grandchild reference caused Harry to puzzle over the words for a few seconds. "Whose baby died, Mother?"

Victoria's eyes began to close as the word tumbled out of her mouth. "Yours." With that, she was asleep again.

"Mine." Harry spoke the word aloud and felt the echo bounce off the walls of the silent room. She then whispered the word again. "Mine."

Harry's mind tumbled over something she had considered fleetingly moments earlier. Now, it appeared a fact. This was about her, Abby, and their baby.

"What did that bastard do?" Her anger was quickly coursing through her veins. For years, she had suffered from the guilt of not being with Abby for that check up. And, now there was a possibility that she had been the intended victim after all. Her guilt went up a thousand fold.

Harry felt the trickle of tears. How could she fight something that had haunted her for years but never actually made sense? Now, it made perfect sense. For some reason her mother had been embroiled with someone who had exacted a price that was beyond redemption. They had wanted her dead and instead had taken Abby and the unborn child they had so wanted, not to mention Sam. "Why?"

The bottom line was unmistakable—she should be dead and not Abby or the baby. Some pervert had wanted to teach her mother a lesson by inflicting the worse possible pain—the death of a child. Only they hadn't managed to kill the right person. "The question now is why didn't they try again? Who other than my mother would know? Maybe Steven?"

What had she ever done to warrant not only abandonment by the woman who called herself her mother but also being instrumental in the death of her partner and their unborn child? This wasn't right. It couldn't be. "Life isn't that cruel, is it?"

Lauren and Nicky entered the room giggling as two old friends do.

Nicky immediately stopped when heard Harry's last words. "Is everything okay, Harry?" Nicky walked over with a bag.

Harry turned toward them unable to smile or even answer Nicky. Her skin felt stretched beyond breaking point.

"Something is terribly wrong here. What is it Harry?" Nicky touched Harry's shoulder. "Tell me what has happened."

"I need some air." Harry stood up.

"Is Victoria okay?" Nicky asked.

Harry shied away from the two women.

"Harry?" Lauren frowned "Tell me what's happened."

"She is ... the other's weren't so lucky." Harry strode out of the room unable to say more.

∞

Nicky looked at Victoria, who appeared to be sleeping peacefully. Her mother confirmed there might be the odd, occasional ramble but nothing that would be worrisome. Victoria was on the mend.

Lauren touched Nicky's arm. "Go with her, Nic. Make her open up to you even if she doesn't want to."

"I've never seen her like this before, Lori. What if she won't speak to me?"

"Then you stay with her until she does. She shouldn't be alone."

Bewildered at what had happened she clutched the bag that still held the bagel and grabbed the cup with the coffee. "I ... we'll be back as soon as possible." Nicky gave Lori a trembling smile and left the room.

∞

Lauren made her way over to the bed and took her mother's hand. "What happened here, Mom? Why is Harry in such a state?"

Victoria stirred and mumbled so softly that Lauren had to lean in to hear her. "My grandchild, he took my grandchild."

Lauren frowned. *"Grandchild? Does my mom have another son or daughter waiting in the wings?"* Then she realized why Harry was so upset. "Oh my, God. Oh, Harry, no wonder you were like that."

∞

Nicky rushed out of the room scanning the corridor. She didn't see Harry anywhere. At the nurse's station, she saw Nurse Hatcher. "Have you seen my friend?"

"She looked very upset and went toward the elevators."

"Thank you." Nicky went to the window and waited a couple of minutes before she saw Harry walking out of the building and going toward the garden. Nicky, deciding to walk instead of taking the elevator, hurried down the stairwell. She needed to think fast on how to approach Harry.

As she neared Harry, Nicky sighed. When were they ever going to have a time when friction and emotional distress wasn't coming in their direction?

"Do you mind if I sit?" Silence was the only reply. She took Harry's silence as a maybe, sat down, and discreetly observed her. *She looks so lost and alone.* Nicky silently beseeched Harry to acknowledge her presence. "I thought you might need coffee." She placed the container on the bench between them so Harry could take it or not.

The silence deepened.

Nicky twisted her hands in her lap and bit down on her lip and wished she hadn't when she unexpectedly drew blood causing her to cry out.

Harry turned to her with a questioning glance.

Nicky noted the bleakness within the depths of her expressive eyes.

"Are you okay?"

Whatever was bothering Harry didn't exclude her. Nicky took that as a plus and smiled. "I bit my lip and it hurt."

Ice blue eyes zeroed in on the lips. "Why?"

"I'm worried about you, Harry. Will you let me help you?"

"You can't help me, Nicky. No one can. It's too late for that. I should be dead."

The bleakness of the words pierced Nicky's heart. "How can you say that? There's no reason to think that."

"You don't know and I don't want to tell you."

Nicky moved until she was as close as possible to Harry. "Please, tell me what or who is hurting you like this, Harry. We can work it out together just as we always have. We're that invincible team ... don't you remember that?"

Tears slowly trickled down Harry's cheeks. "It's too late. I'm so sorry."

"Hey, everything is going to be fine, I promise you." Nicky tenderly placed her arms about Harry expecting resistance but was surprised to find that Harry sank into her like a distraught child. For several minutes, Nicky held Harry close, soothing her with gentle words, tenderly stroking her hair with the occasional kiss to the top of her head. Her tears were slowly trailing down her cheeks. It was killing her not knowing what the problem was but eventually she would find out. She had to be patient. At times like this, Harry couldn't be hurried.

"I should be the one dead, Nicky, and not your sister, the baby or Sam. The accident was meant for me and not them, I should be dead."

"Harry, please, you're not making sense. Who told you that evil rubbish?" Nicky was distraught. *How can anyone say such cruel words? Hasn't Harry paid enough over the years for Abby's death?* It was an accident and not Harry's fault.

"It isn't evil, Nicky. My mother told me. The guy who died—that mayor—he arranged it. She told me."

Nicky pulled her lover closer trying to protect her from the stupid comments. "Victoria did? She was rambling, Harry. It is the drug. My mother ..."

213

"No. I believe her." The words echoed ominously between them.

"Then we will work it out when she's more lucid. Let's go back and see how she's doing?" Nicky wasn't convinced about the story. Victoria was probably rambling. It would be common for someone in her condition. Who knew what the effects the drug had? She certainly didn't.

Harry pulled away abruptly.

Nicky saw Harry's face was full of pain and something that Nicky didn't grasp.

"How can you expect me to go back? If it weren't for that woman, Abby would still be alive. We would have a child and still be together?"

Nicky reeled from the statement and clenched at her stomach. "I didn't realize that you felt like that, Harry."

"How do you expect me to feel? Don't you loathe her too? Your sister died because of her."

Nicky struggled to understand all the undercurrents Harry's words threw into their relationship. She stood. "You need to talk with Victoria when she feels better to get the full story. She could be hallucinating. We don't know how the drug affects people yet. This could be a side effect. I refuse to judge someone who is as sick as she is. Perhaps you could do the same."

"I could, but if there is even a half truth there I don't want anything to do with her. She has caused enough pain in my life already. Surely you can understand that."

"I do and I feel sorry for you. Harry. No, I feel sorry for us." Her eyes trained on the green foliage in front of them. For a few moments, she could imagine herself back in the splendor of the jungle and its relative simplicity of life in comparison to what went on in this concrete jungle.

"Is there still an *us*?"

Nicky spun around to face Harry. "How dare you ask that of me, Harry! Of course there is. How can you think otherwise? The bottom line is I love you and even if you don't love me the same way I'm willing to take what crumbs of affection you can give me. If you want me to beg you to love me a little I will gladly do it."

"I don't love you in the same way as you love me, Nicky," Harry responded.

A startled look overran Nicky's features.

Harry stood and pulled Nicky's stiff body into her arms. "I love you more. So much so that I feel as guilty as hell that I'm alive and filled with so much joy at having you in my life and that Abby is gone. Should this be happening? Can I have this much happiness at the expense of your sister's life?"

Nicky now understood the problem. It wasn't Harry's resurrected love of Abby. It was that their love was all consuming and Harry felt guilty that she had this measure of happiness in her life.

"My sister loved you, Harry. You and she were happy and would have been together now if the tragedy hadn't occurred. All I know is that fate put us in places that allowed us to fall in love and I'm not going to let it go. You're going to have to divorce me first."

For the first time in a while, Harry smiled. It was a small one, but it glimmered there nonetheless. "You need to marry me first."

They stared into each other eyes, lost in a world of their own and Nicky grinned. "I'll think about it when we get home,"

"I'll hold you to that. I guess we need to go back now."

"Not if you don't want to. I'll go alone if you prefer."

"What did you say earlier? We make an invincible team. I know you're right. Let's get the full story shall we? Together we'll decide how it affects our future."

"You got that right, Harry." Nicky held out her hand and they walked back toward the hospital and the truth.

∞

Lauren stood at the window watching Harry sitting on a bench. She looked so isolated there even though plants and other visitors to the garden surrounded her. She saw Nicky walked to the bench, only to stand there seemingly unsure. When she saw them embrace, she was glad her sister had such a wonderful loving person in her life.

Victoria began to stir once more as Lauren noted it was time for another dose of medicine. She walked over to the bed. Her mother's eyes were open and focusing on her.

"Hey, how are you feeling?"

Victoria giggled. "Like hell."

Lauren smiled at the comment. That was so very much like her mother. "Not surprised, I think you may have been there and back." Lauren pressed the syringe into the IV site. "We need to do some blood work and tests but I think you've weathered the worst of the storm."

"Between storms and hell I must be looking rather ravishing."

"Mom, believe me when I tell you that no matter what you have been through you always manage to look beautiful."

"That she always does." Steven was standing in the doorway with a big smile on his face. "So, I see my girl is finally awake." He walked over to the bed, bent down, and gave her a gentle kiss. "Good to have you back." Steven looked at his daughter. "Thanks for calling me."

Victoria took her husband's hand. "I will always come back to you." Her eyes focused on Lori. "Something happened here but I can't remember what. It was important though. Was Harry here?"

"Yeah, she's here, Mom." She looked out the window and noticed the empty bench. "They should be back shortly."

"Good. I wish could remember." Victoria closed her eyes and fell back to sleep.

"Lori?"

"Don't worry, Dad. She will go in and out for some time yet before she is completely cognizant. Right now, we need to watch her carefully for any adverse effects to the drug. Nicky's mother said this would be the most critical time."

When she heard voices, Lauren turned to see her sister and dear friend standing in the hallway.

"Nicky, I can't go in there now. I just can't."

"Hey, remember we are in this together. I won't let you down, Harry."

"Please, Nic, give me some more time."

Lauren couldn't help but overhear the conversation. Harry, as she suspected, was angry. Who could blame her?

"Hi, you two. Glad you came back. Mom has been asking for you, Harry." Lauren could see the stress on her sister's face. How she wanted to just hug her close and make it all right for her. "Nicky, the course of the treatment seems to be going along just as your mother predicted. Another twenty-four and I think we will see lasting results."

"Are the latest workups back yet? I think they will tell us a great deal, don't you?" Nicky moved closer to Harry and took her hand.

"They should be here anytime now. Harry, may I ask a big favor of you?"

"It depends on the favor, Lori." Harry looked at her sister.

"As you know, Maggie's mother is here, but she needs to go back to the hotel and get freshened up. Is there any chance I might persuade you to go and sit with Maggie until her mother gets back?"

"No problem, Lori. Want me to go there now?"

This time Lauren couldn't help herself. She walked over to Harry and engulfed her in a big hug. "Yes. Thank you."

Harry stood like a statue and then returned the hug.

Chapter Twenty-six

Caroline looked up from her book to see a strikingly beautiful woman enter the room. "Do I know you? You look very familiar to me."

"Harry, Lauren is my sister."

"Oh, yes, Lauren. What a wonderful girl. Sure thought I knew you, guess you look like someone I know. It will come to me." Caroline got up from her chair to shake the woman's hand.

"I don't think we've met before. I'm usually good at remembering people."

Caroline looked intently at the woman. Lauren is her sister. *That's it. She's Vicky's girl.* "Have you come to visit with Meg? She's asleep right now, I'm afraid."

"I've come to relieve you. Lauren tells me you need to visit the hotel and freshen up. I'm the cavalry. Maggie knows me. She will be safe with me."

"Well, cavalry, you couldn't have come at a more opportune moment. It will take some time getting use to calling my Meg, Maggie. I remember who you remind me of—you are the spitting image of your mother." A warm smile crossed Carolyn's face, as she knew the significance of this to her friend, Vicky.

"You know my mother?" Harry asked.

Caroline tipped her head and studied the woman who reminded her so much of her college friend. "Yes, we went to Harvard together. We all did. At one time, we were going to set up practice together but we were not destined to do that. Steven married

Vicky, and I married Patrick. We went our own ways yet kept in touch. You do bare a remarkable resemblance to your mother."

"A chip off the old block some say. Well, I won't keep you, Mrs. Connelly. The sooner you go the sooner you get back to Maggie. I'm sure she will prefer your company to mine when she wakes."

Caroline picked up immediately on the tone of Harry's words. "Is something wrong, dear? Has your mother taken a turn for the worse?" For some reason Caroline felt compelled to hug this woman and she did. "Want to talk about it?"

Harry stiffened in the embrace. "No, my mother is doing well and I'm fine. Thanks for asking. It's been a long day. So much going on and more to come, I'm sure."

"You poor child. How confused you must be by all of this. Your mother and I have been close friends for a long time. I can remember her sobbing long into the night when she first told me about you. And now, here you are in this place watching a stranger really, fight for her life." Caroline patted Harry's arm. "I am a very good listener, dear. Maybe I could fill in some of the blanks for you."

"She cried … for me? I find that hard to believe under the circumstances of my birth."

"Of course she cried for you dear. She loves you and always has."

Harry's reaction wasn't unexpected. Caroline knew of all that surrounded Vicky's decision of not to take her daughter from her uncle.

"She could have fooled me … no, strike that, she did fool me. Hey, but what the hell, it was years ago. We all move on."

Caroline saw the anger in Harry's face but saw something else—sadness. "Do you have any idea what your mother went through to keep you safe? The sole purpose of getting a law degree was to find a way to get you back. Every time she tried, your uncle would put her off, and then threaten to leave the country with you. Knowing you were at least in the same country was better than not knowing where you were at all, Harry."

"I'm aware of my uncle's tactics. Understandably he didn't want to lose me either. After all, he did bring me up from a baby. Who could blame him? I certainly wouldn't and haven't."

"But, you can't bring yourself to forgive your mother, can you?" Caroline moved closer to Harry. "A mother's love runs deep and long, dear. She was willing to give you up rather than to have you face a long, ugly court battle."

Harry shrugged. "Why should I believe you? As you said, my mother is little more than a stranger to me."

"Tell me, Harriet, what would you have done if the situation were reversed?"

"As in, I had abandoned my child?"

"Yes, when you were but a child yourself."

"I wouldn't have done what she did. I understand responsibility. I always have. No child of mine would ever feel abandoned. It wouldn't happen."

"Never? Are you sure of that? What would you do if the circumstances made it impossible for you to keep your child? What would you do if it were out of your control, Harry? What if, no matter what you did, there would never be a way to take it back or make it right?" Caroline's heart went out to the sad, lonely woman whose heart was obviously breaking.

"I've already been there, Mrs. Connelly, and it hurts like the bowels of hell. One day my child might forgive me too. I have to hope for that in the next life."

Harry's words were so soft that Caroline barely heard them. "Your child?"

Harry turned to the woman with a tight lipped expression. "I thought you and my mother were close confidantes? Surely she told you that she was expecting a grandchild a few years back?"

A nurse entered the room. "Would you do me a favor, dear, and stay here with my daughter until I get back?" Once she was confident someone would look after Meg, Caroline took Harry by the hand and led her out to the waiting room. "I think you need to sit down for this, Harry."

"Look, why should I sit? You think my mother can do no wrong and at this moment I think the reverse."

"Please, hear me out. I know better than to think your mother can do no wrong. You need answers, Harry, and I have them. If you will just sit and listen. Please."

"Go ahead, I'm listening." Harry sat ridged.

"Early on, your mother never told anyone about you except her uncle. One day the old man let it slip to someone and that started a chain of events that has led to this day." Caroline stopped and looked into Harry's eyes to see if she understood. "This man eventually became the mayor of a small, but very rich town. Once in office, he seized the opportunity to use his knowledge to manipulate your mother. For years she pretended to go along with him but never did anything illegal or unethical." Caroline sighed heavily.

"Go on."

"The mayor fell in with a rather unsavory faction and a plan was hatched to transform the lovely town of Warwick into a shopping Mecca. He, of course, needed the town's approval and that meant your mother. She wanted nothing to do with it and told him so. That was ten months ago." Her eyes were distant as she recalled the dilemma her friend found herself in. "The Mayor threatened to expose her but she told him to go ahead because she wasn't going to let him destroy the town. It was then that he pulled out a tattered newspaper clipping about an accident that happened five years earlier." Caroline looked at Harry to gauge whether to go on or not.

"Carry on, please."

Caroline moved closer to Harry and took her hand in hers. "He told her he could kill her daughter and Vicky scoffed at him. Then he gave her the article and told her that he missed killing you that time but wouldn't again. And, he indicated he might just do Lori in for good measure. When your mother read the article, she knew what had happened. Yes, she knew you lost your partner and child, but never dreamt it was anything more than an accident." Caroline could feel Harry trembling. She moved closer and put her arm around her shoulders. "It was then that she set in motion a plan to foil the mayor and save her daughters."

"I don't think I can take any more in. This is too much," Harry whispered.

Carline pulled Harry closer still and soothed her hair. "Let it go, Harry. Let it all go." Then she began singing a soft lullaby and rocked Harry gently as a mother would her child.

"I can't. Don't you see? I can't. I should be the one dead. Not Abby or our child. How can I live with the knowledge that they died because of me. It was hard enough rebuilding my life when I thought it was an accident. Now, that I know it was deliberate and was aimed at me how do I live with myself."

Caroline kissed the head in her arms. "You know, Harry, in life many things happen to us and to those we love. Many times, we ask why and have no answers but we carry on because there really isn't another choice. Out of your grief, you found a great love. Out of your grief, you found your mother. Out of your grief, you found a sister. Are they not reason enough to go on?" Caroline hugged Harry closer still. "How do you think your mother lives with herself? When the mayor shot her, she took it as her penance for you losing your family. I suspect she blames herself more than you ever will or can."

"I wouldn't want to live without Nicky. She's my life. I feel guilty because I love Nicky so much more than I did Abby. Perhaps out of senseless tragedy you get second chances, I'll have to consider that more often. Thank you, Mrs. Connelly. I appreciate your frankness. I don't think I would have listened to this from anyone I know."

Caroline looked fondly at the woman. "Dear, you are most welcome and please, call me Caroline."

Harry smiled.

"Do you think you could still stay with my Meg while I go back to the hotel?"

"Of course. You go ahead and take your time. She'll be in good hands, I promise."

Harry and the woman stood.

"Thank you. I won't be long." Carolyn began to exit the room then turned. "Harry, life isn't what happens to you. It is what you learn from it."

"Yes, it is," whispered Harry.

∞

Harry's mind seemed at peace for the first time in she couldn't even remember when. Having finally said the words, 'I love Nicky more than I did Abby', made her realize that it was time to set her priorities. The number one mission would be Nicky.

"What are you doing here? Where's my mom?"

Maggie's voice broke Harry's reverie. "She went back to the hotel for a little while so you got me by default. Trust me; I don't want to be here anymore than you want me here."

"Look, Harry, we got off to a bad start from the beginning. What do you say we start again?" A slight smile crossed Maggie's lips. "Hi, Harry. Thank you for being here with me."

Harry looked at the woman and for some unknown reason couldn't help smiling. "Glad I could be of help. Do you need anything? Water, food, wine, woman? I see by the tray here you have a wonderful assortment of … hmmm … looks like … yep … mush. Yummy."

Maggie grimaced but then laughed. "Think I will pass on that one. I could use some help going to the bathroom. Could you ring the nurse for me?"

"Like they will come before your bladder explodes. Why not let me help you." Harry was out of her element but she promised Caroline she would be here for Maggie and that was exactly what she intended to do.

Maggie swung her legs as best she could over the side of the bed ready to slide off and stand. Harry put an arm around her.

"Lean on me, Maggie."

"Thanks, we need to take the IV with us too." They shuffled together toward the bathroom.

After the jaunt to the bathroom, Maggie sat in a chair. "Harry, thank you."

"You're welcome." Harry tried to recall why they were such adversaries. "Maggie, I didn't know our mothers knew each other."

Maggie's eyebrows furrowed. "I think you must be mistaken, Harry. I never met Victoria before I came here. Whatever gave you that idea?"

Harry studied Maggie's expressions and gestures for some sort of deception. "You didn't know they were friends?"

"They're not, as far as I know."

"Maggie, your mother just told me they went to law school together." Harry could see the confusion and doubt in Maggie's eyes. If she was pretending, she was one fine actress.

"In my father's line of work, it doesn't pay to advertise who your friends are,"

Harry's curiosity was peeked now. "What exactly *does* your father do?"

"If I told you I would have to kill you."

A shiver went up Harry's spine. "Yes, I believe you would." Harry studied Maggie and her eyes went wide. "Maggie, what's wrong? Are you in pain? Do you want me to get the doctor?"

"Lauren. Does Lauren know?" Maggie was visibly shaking.

"Know? Know what?"

"About our mother's friendship? Harry, I need to find her." Maggie began to stand.

Harry put her hand on Maggie's shoulder and gently pushed her back in the chair. "Maggie, sit back down. Relax. I will get a wheelchair and we will go find Lori. I don't know if she knows or not but I rather doubt it."

"Please, will you get the wheelchair? I need to see her now."

Harry uncharacteristically, patted Maggie's shoulder. "Will you promise to stay put until I find the chair?"

Maggie nodded.

"Good, I will be right back."

∞

Nicky and Lauren were huddled together reading the test results. "This is unbelievable, Lori. Wait until my mother gets this news. Never in our wildest dreams did we think this would happen."

"Can you believe it, Nic? The possibilities are limitless. God, I can't believe I am part of something this monumental. As a researcher this is the chance of a lifetime." Lauren looked over the results once again and grinned. "Yep, those are the results. Do you think we should run them again, just to be sure?"

Nicky glanced at the results. "It wouldn't hurt, Lori. I can't wait until we can publish this."

Lori saw a goofy expression on Nicky's face and figured she didn't need to turn around to see her sister. "Someone special coming, Nicky?"

Nicky turned her head back toward her friend and winked. "Two someone special, Lori."

Lori's heart did flips. The most glorious sight she could imagine was her sister helping Maggie. "Hey, you two. Did you get a pass from your doctor to be out and about?" She bent down to kiss the cheek of her lover.

"Lauren, we need to talk," Maggie said.

"And we shall, but first we have great news." Lauren's enthusiasm for the test results didn't allow her to see the urgency of Maggie's request.

"Harry, you are not going to believe what has happened. Your mother's kidneys have begun to function again." Nicky took Harry's hand.

"That's impossible. Did it really happen? How? Why? When? I don't understand," Harry said.

"Lauren, I really need to speak with you right now."

Lauren was beaming with delight. Everything was coming together; everything was going to be okay. Out of the corner of her eye, she saw Caroline exiting the elevator and smiled happily. Then she heard the urgency in Maggie's voice but didn't understand the words. She bent down and looked at the face she realized had stress written all over it. "Maggie, are you okay? Is something wrong?"

"I need to be alone with you, *now*, Lauren. Please."

The joy Lauren was feeling was gone, replaced with concern. At the same time, the tone of Maggie's voice terrified her. "Of course. We can go back to your room." She moved behind the wheelchair. "Harry, I'm taking Maggie back now. We will talk more when I return."

∞

Harry discreetly watched her sister's and Maggie's body language. Something was up and it had to do with their mothers. Of that, she was sure. Seeing Caroline walking toward them, she made a decision. "You two go on now." Once they were moving away, Harry turned to the woman who just exited the elevator. "Caroline, welcome back. Have you met my partner, Nicky Ralston?"

Caroline smiled at Nicky. "Well, yes and no. I have met her but not formally." She held out her. "Hi, Nicky, I am Caroline Connelly, Meg ... I mean Maggie's mother."

"Hello, it's wonderful to meet you. Will you please excuse me? I see more test results have come back." Nicky squeezed Harry's forearm and winked. "I won't be long."

Harry watched Nicky walk away for a few seconds before she turned to Caroline. "I think we need to talk."

∞

Lauren wheeled Maggie into her room all the while her mind filled with the anxiety of the unknown. She thought back and couldn't recall a time when she saw Maggie in such a state.

Once in her hospital room, Maggie sighed. "Would you close the door please, Lauren?"

After closing the door, Lauren moved in front of Maggie and crouched down so they would be at eye level. "You're frightening me. Please tell me what is going on. Did Doctor Green have bad news for you? Did Harry do or say something to upset you? Please, I need to know."

"Lauren, do you know how much I love you?"

Maggie seemed defeated and tired to Lauren. *She's gone through so much with her injuries that I bet this is just too much for her.* "Yes, I do. I know I have neglected you and probably have made you feel unloved. But, that is not, nor could ever be, the case. If I promise to spend more time with you, will you forgive me? I love you, Maggie, with all my heart and soul."

"Lauren, you don't understand. I need you to know before I tell you that I didn't know. I swear."

Lauren creased her forehead. "Okay. I feel like I'm out of the loop because I haven't a clue about what you are telling me. I trust and believe in you so please tell me what is going on."

"My mother …"

∞

Harry took Caroline's arm and steering her toward a quiet area of the corridor.

"Is there something you wanted to say, Harriet?"

"Well, it's more what you can tell me."

"That would be?"

"Maggie didn't know about you and my mother being friends did she?" Harry gave the older woman a shrewd glance. She would know if Maggie's mother lied to her—she always knew.

"No. No she didn't. I learned a long time ago that it was prudent to keep friends separate in my life."

There was sadness about the statement that touched Harry—she knew how that worked. "Even from family?"

"Particularly from family, trust me on that one. You have heard the phrase 'on a need to know basis,' that works where my family is concerned."

"What do you mean? Don't you trust your family with your friends or vice versa?"

Caroline let out a soft chuckle at the question. "Actually, the phrase 'if I told you, I would have to kill you' comes to mind when you divulge anything with my family."

The term rang loud bells in Harry's mind. *Isn't that exactly how Maggie termed it?* Now Maggie was going to spill the beans to Lauren and it wasn't necessary. The mist that had shrouded her cleared suddenly, as she realized the implications of knowing too much about Maggie's family.

"Caroline, why don't you go visit with Vicky and Steven. They have something wonderful to tell you." Harry turned on her heel and headed for Maggie's room.

∞

Harry went in without knocking and heard Maggie say 'My mother …"

"Her mother is one fine lady and she wants to know why you both ignored her when she came back?" Harry stood inside the doorway with a smug smile on her face and arms crossed over her chest.

"Harry, what are you doing here?" Lauren asked.

"I'm here to tell you that you need to speak with Caroline. It's that simple."

"It can wait, my mother will understand."

"Perhaps, however I won't. Anyway, there is someone else who would like to meet you." Harry wondered why she said that for she hadn't a clue who to say wanted to meet them.

"Okay, who?"

For a few seconds Harry faced them both and was about to laugh and try a joke when she felt a hand on her shoulder. She turned and stared into the familiar features of someone she loved dearly. "Uncle Harry." Harriet hugged the frail older gentleman and felt the tears prick at her eyelids. *What impeccable timing.*

"I love you too, Harriet. Sorry I came out of the blue like this but I wanted to see Victoria." The old man's eyes twinkled.

"It's good to see you. Now, I'd like you to meet my sister Lauren and her partner, Maggie."

Harry Aristides smiled and nodded at Lauren, "Ms. Walker and I are acquainted. Maggie, I'm very happy to make your acquaintance." He walked over and held out his hand.

"Pleased to meet you too, Mr. Aristides."

Lauren sidled over to her sister. "Why is he here?"

Harry lifted her hands. "Don't know. He said he wanted to speak with Victoria."

"Our mother won't see him. She doesn't like him and in her fragile state, seeing him might be detrimental to her."

"Well, we will find out, won't we?" Harry strode across to Maggie out of Lauren's earshot.

"Don't tell her about your mother's friendship with Victoria. It serves no purpose."

"Okay, but I need to tell her. I promised no secrets and that is what I'll do."

Harry nodded and then turned to her uncle. "Well, Uncle Harry, if you want to see Victoria, I think I can arrange that." She placed her arm around her uncle's shoulder and steered him to the door

232

leaving the other two occupants of the room to wonder what was going on.

∞

"I think you can tell me what you need to say, Maggie." Lauren laughed. "Can you believe what is going on? Please tell me and then we can go see how the reunion of Uncle Harry and my mother goes."

"Okay. Apparently, your mother and mine went to Harvard together. I just found that out when my mom revealed that fact to Harry."

Lauren smiled and placed a light kiss on Maggie's lips. "Can this day get any more bizarre? Oh, guess what? My mom's kidneys are working again."

"Really? That is wonderful." Maggie let out a laugh and instantly pain creased her face. "I don't think bizarre covers it. Let's go find our mothers." She chuckled as Lauren began to push the wheelchair. "Let's see if I got this straight. First, unexpectedly my mother comes to the hospital, then ..."

∞

After opening the door to the hospital room, Harry smiled at her uncle bemused by his appearance and his desire to see her mother. As the door opened wide, she saw Steven talking to Caroline and Nicky was watching over Victoria. *This should be interesting.*

Nicky turned at the sound of the door and her smile beamed. "Hi, is everything okay with Maggie?"

Harry grinned back. For some reason, having her uncle here to meet Nicky gave her a sense of euphoria that she hadn't felt before. It was like finally allowing the final barrier of her life to fall.

"She's great. Nic, I need you to do something for me."

"Anything, you know that. What can I do?"

"Would you please take Steven and Caroline for a coffee or something to eat for say half an hour? It's important."

Nicky glanced at the older man, who gave her a smile. "Of course."

"Steven, how about grabbing some coffee with me. Harry's here and she'll call us if Victoria wakes."

Steven turned to look at Harry and the man with her.

"Hey, Steve, want to buy me a cup of coffee? We can talk more there," Caroline said.

"Sure." Steven walked over to the stranger in the room and held out his hand. "Steven Walker."

The man took the proffered hand. "Harry Aristides."

Steven let his hand drop. "What are *you* doing here?"

"I'm old and I'm dying and wanted to make things right with Victoria." Harry's voice quavered.

"You've kept her from her daughter for over forty years and you now want redemption for your past sins." Steven shook his head. "Not while I'm alive."

Harriet moved between the two men. "Please, Steven, let him speak to her. I'll stay here the whole time and won't let any harm come to Victoria."

Steven wiped a hand down his face. "Only because it is you asking will I allow him to speak with my wife, Harriet. Don't let me down."

"I won't. I promise."

Caroline hooked her arm in Steven's and led him toward the door. "There's a wonderful coffee shop two blocks down. Let's go there?" Caroline stopped for a moment to squeeze Harry's forearm and smile warmly toward her.

"Want me to bring you a latte? Nicky asked.

"Sure and a mocha too." Harry nodded toward her uncle.

"You got it. See you later."

"I meant what I told Steven, Uncle Harry. Please don't make this difficult."

The older man's eyes hadn't left the sleeping form in the bed from the first moment he came into the room. "That was never my intention, Harriet. I simply wanted to see your mother and ..."

Victoria stirred. "Harry?" She first gazed at her daughter then at the older gentleman.

"Yes." Both man and woman spoke at the same time.

"Mother, my uncle is here to see you."

Her eyes fixed on the man. "*You.* What are *you* doing here? How dare you come here?"

Harry Aristides drew back his shoulders. "Yes, it's me, Vicky."

Harriet sucked in a breath as she realized the stupidity of allowing her uncle to visit her mother. Victoria's agitation was evident and Harriet was desperate to get her uncle out of the room.

Before she could make her move, Victoria lashed out again.

"Haven't you caused me enough sorrow? Are you here in hopes of seeing me die? Sorry to disappoint you."

Harriet watched the exchange as if a movie scene was unfolding. She grabbed her uncle's arm. "We should go."

Harry pulled his arm away from her hold. "You know that isn't the case, Vicky, how could I? Don't you remember when we first met?"

"I remember only too well, Harry. What do you want? You have always wanted something."

"The only thing I ever wanted, Vicky, was you."

Harriet gasped as she heard the words. *What does this mean? My uncle is actually secretly in love with my mother. Is that why he never married?*

"How dare you, Harry."

"I dare because you know it's true. You've always known. That's why you left Harriet with me in the first place."

"I was sixteen years old, Harry. I clearly told you when I was twenty-three, that there was no future for us.

"I know that and I've always known that this time around, we were never meant to be together." He nodded toward Harriet. "She's like you in many ways. I'm proud to have spent my life with her. To me she's the daughter I secretly hoped I would have with you. To all intents and purposes she is. I love her very much."

Harriet choked on the words. "Do you love me because of my mother or for me, as myself?"

Harry turned. "I love you for who you have become to me, Harriet. Believe me you are one of a kind."

"Are you okay, Harry? You don't look well."

Harry glanced at his niece to silence her. "Quite all right. Thank you, Vicky. Time hasn't been kind to me as it has to you."

"All that running around has finally caught up to you, Harry. You look like hell." Harry heard her mother's words and felt the anger dissipate and instead there was pity in her tone.

At the doorway, a stunned Lauren and Maggie listened to the exchange.

"Maybe we should go," Maggie whispered.

"Not yet. I need to hear this. I need to know."

"May I ask a question?" Harriet asked.

Harry glanced at his niece. "Yes."

"Ask anything you want, Harriet." Victoria smiled warmly.

"How much do you love my mother, Harry? How much do you hate Harry, Mother?"

"That's two questions, Harriet." Harry managed a smile.

"Yeah, but it is special circumstances."

Harold Aristides smiled. "You are something else, Harriet."

"Sweetheart, I used to hate him as no other. Now, I only pity him for the ruse he has perpetrated on you for all these years. How terrified he must have been that you would leave him if he told you the truth. You are my child and you are loyal to a fault. That I know."

"I've loved your mother from the first, Harriet. She was fifteen years old and we saw her at the state fair. Your father was far more confident than I was and asked her out even though he knew I liked her. That was his way."

Victoria listened to his words and her mind flashed back to the first time she saw Rob Aristides. Harry paled in comparison; she never would have been interested in him. *He showed his love for me by holding Harriet hostage all these years.* "Tell me,

Harry, if you loved me so much why did you deny me my daughter? You knew how much I wanted her, yet you blocked my every attempt to get her back. Why?" If Victoria was ever to forgive the man, she needed that question answered.

"How can you ask me that, Vicky? She was six months old when you left her with me and it was five years later when you asked for her back. I knew more of her than you did. I went through her first steps, words, and laughter. Can you say the same?" His voice was raspy. "Of course, my other option was adoption thereby leaving you out in the cold."

"Not good enough, Harry. I was in contact with you from the time Rob died. You knew what my circumstances were and why I couldn't have her back then. I always made it clear to you I wanted my daughter back one day. So again I ask, *why*?"

"She is my daughter. I don't care what you say. By the time, you decided you wanted her back she had become my life. By then, I wanted to keep her. I loved her it was as simple as that. It doesn't take DNA to say she's mine, Vicky, it takes love."

"So do I, Harry. You denied me the opportunity of showing her my love, of knowing her love, and of our being mother and daughter. Do you have any idea the hell I went through on birthdays and holidays? Did you even care?"

"Enough to keep everything you sent."

Victoria shook her head and once again looked at the man. "She never got them? You hated me so much that you denied her my gifts!"

"There is a simple question for you to answer here, Vicky. If you loved her that much why did you leave her with me? I was a bachelor."

"Most of the time I could never find you and when I did, you would disappear, Harry. It wasn't my choice, you made sure of that."

"What a load of rubbish, Vicky. Every time you called I always came didn't I?"

"Sure, when I could find you. Do you consider yourself completely innocent of any guilt in this?"

"No. I realized too late that she needed you in her life. By then you had a husband and a child." He lifted a thin shoulder. "I thought it would be okay. I thought you didn't want her any more. I'm sorry."

As a sense of letting go came over Victoria and she felt relief. "Listen, Harry, we both had our hearts in the right place. Unfortunately, we never listened to each other. A husband and a child never made up for the loss of my child. It only added to the pain." Victoria looked at Harriet and smiled. "What do you say we just let it all go for our daughter's sake? How horrible this must be for her."

"I let go a long time ago, Vicky. I loved you then, I love you now, and I love our daughter more. I came here to tell you so."

Victoria closed her eyes. For the first time in forty years, she felt a weight lift from her heart. "Harriet, I have always loved you. We lost forty years due to pride and stubbornness. Do you think we can start again? Can we have any type of relationship? I can't begin to tell you how I have longed for that."

"I think we might have all the time in the world to start again—the three of us." Harriet smiled first toward her mother then her uncle.

Tears were now flowing out of not only Victoria's eyes, but out of both her daughters. "Thank you." She glanced past Harry and noticed Lauren and

Maggie in the doorway. "It looks like we have visitors."

Yes, everything was going to work out now. Nothing would stand in the way of her family finally coming together. And, if that family included Harold Aristides, it was not only fine, but also appropriate. As she welcomed them inside, she couldn't help the smile growing wider as she saw Nicky struggling with two obviously warm cups as she entered the room.

"Ah, just the person I wanted to see." Harry walked over to Nicky and took the latte from her.

Nicky grinned. "I love you too, Harry. Now, who wants the mocha?"

"Since you asked, I think my uncle would like it. I know you don't know him but you will. Shall we have dinner together tonight?"

"Great."

The room filled with positive energy that flowed into each of their hearts. For the first time, in what seemed like forever, everything was coming together. The future was bright for them all.

Chapter Twenty-seven

Harry considered herself a reasonably open-minded woman in most things, but she reluctantly admitted not everything. But, the bombshell her uncle had exploded in her mother's room had given her food for thought. Now they were on the way back to the hotel to have dinner with that very person. Her uncle was to leave the following morning and this would be the only chance for him to get to know Nicky.

Nicky's initial introduction was brief, as events were unfolding rapidly at the time. Harry would make sure to rectify that at dinner. When she glanced in her uncle's direction, she noticed he was deep in thought as well.

Upon entering the hotel, Harry smiled at Nicky who had remained silent. As always, Nicky knew something was wrong but would wait until Harry decided to open up.

"How about we freshen up and meet in the lobby for dinner? Say in half an hour?"

Nicky immediately nodded agreement and the old man smiled faintly. "Sure, I'll see you then."

Harriet asked for the key to their room and then booked a room for her uncle.

"I'll go shower while you settle your uncle." Nicky took the key from Harry and received a grateful smile.

"Thanks, Nic. I'll get another key and make sure I make some noise when I get there." Harry grinned as the smaller woman left them and disappeared inside the elevator that had conveniently appeared as if on cue.

"Madam, here is the key to the gentlemen's room." Harry smiled at the stubby man and took the key. "When I come back I will need another key to my room."

"Very well."

"All ready, Uncle Harry, let's go."

"You know, I don't have to stay at the same hotel, Harriet. You might have wanted some personal space from me."

"I might, then again, I might not. Come on or neither of us will have time for a shower. I can assure you Nicky would have something to say about having dinner with a couple of smelly Aristides." A chuckle and answering smile from her uncle lifted her spirits. They were going to be okay, she knew it. There wasn't time left to bear any grudges. *Then again ... maybe we can do the same thing we did for my mother. We have a powerful drug to help him. I wonder what Nicky will say to this idea?*

∞

"Why not, Nic?" Harry asked desperately for what she thought was the hundredth time.

"I've told you why not. Want me to write it down for you?" Nicky exhaled.

"There's no need for that attitude, Nicky. I was asking a perfectly valid question." Harry sighed.

"Okay, let me say this one more time, and then may we go to dinner. We are already ten minutes late."

"Go ahead." Harry perched on the dressing table in the room they shared.

"The drug isn't approved. Harry, you of all people know what that means. So far, we have managed to keep Victoria's trial and success under wraps. However, if you try it again, there's no certainty that it won't get out. Then what?"

"We can do the same as we did with my mother. In fact, my uncle can stay home and no one else has to know. It should be easier to keep it a secret than in a hospital."

"I know you want to help him. And I do too but we can't. Don't you see that?"

"No. No I don't, Nicky. Call me obtuse or something, but I have the means and access to the drug. It makes sense to me."

Nicky walked over to Harry and gave her a long thoughtful stare. "You can't play God, that's what you would be doing, and for selfish reasons. There are thousands of people dying who need this drug's help, millions probably. If you jeopardize the drug's approval by taking another chance, more than your uncle will die. How would you feel then? I know how I would feel, Harry, it would eat away at me forever and I'd never forgive myself." Nicky hugged Harry.

Harry melted into Nicky's warm embrace. She knew Nicky's warning was stark and factual. They had already taken a big risk by using an untested drug once for personal benefit. To do so twice, was professional suicide and would probably bring about an investigation into Victoria's treatment, and the repercussions for all involved would be colossal. "I guess you are right. I don't want him to die, Nic. He's my family." The emotional upheaval was taking its toll on her in ways she never fathomed. Left behind, was the cold distant Harriet and a new, gentler woman was emerging.

Nicky gently kissed Harry's cheek. "I'll always be here for you, Harry, no matter what."

Harry gulped back the sobs that threatened to break free and smiled into the loving eyes of her partner. "I love you, Nicky. There is no one more important in my life than you. There never will be and there never has been." It was out. She had admitted it and hoped that Nicky understood what she meant. Either way, it was good to say it at last.

"I love you too, Harry. More than you will ever know."

Harry stole a soft passionate kiss. "I know, believe me, I know."

Flushed with the emotions that raged between them, they both pulled away shakily, "I guess we need to have dinner?"

Harry grinned. "I'd love to say let's skip it but …"

"Yeah, I know, your uncle. Do I have the pleasure of meeting him properly now?"

"I'm sorry about earlier. I'll give you a brief version of events as we go down to dinner for you to understand why he wasn't very forthcoming. How would that be?"

Nicky laughing, took Harry's hand as they exited the room, "Harry, do you ever get the feeling life is just one long session of questions?"

Harry chuckled at the truth of the question. "You got that right and some of them don't have answers." They walked down the corridor toward the elevators as Harry began to tell Nicky about her uncle's visit to see Victoria.

∞

As the days passed by, it was evident that Victoria would make a full recovery. The only downside was that until there was proper testing, they could never share their remarkable results.

It was soon time for Harry and Nicky to head back to their home in Houston.

"It's time to go home, Lauren."

Nicky heard Harry's words and saw the surprise mirrored in her friend's face.

"Is there any way I can persuade you to stay longer?" Lauren's asked.

Harry hesitated for a few moments and then shook her head. "I'm sorry, but I'm needed back at the company. We have a wonder drug to keep on track."

"I know."

Nicky's heart went out to the both of them. Even for Harry it would be difficult to leave her family behind. However, Harry was right. They had a drug to keep on track and she suspected that in the ensuing months, it would take up all of Harry's time pushing and cajoling people to work harder than they already did to get it to the approval stage earlier than planned.

Lauren lifted her head and looked at the two women in front of her. "Will you come back for the ceremony?"

"You can always come see us again, just say the word and I'll send the plane for you." Harry said.

Nicky laughed as the two sisters spoke at the same time.

"Without a doubt. You won't keep us away. Right, Harry?"

Harry shrugged. "Sure, all we need is the date."

Lauren paused for a moment. "We haven't set one yet, but I think it will be within the next two months."

A frown appeared on Harry's forehead.

"We will be honored to be there whenever you're ready," Nicky said.

"Yeah, but remember, we need some notice so we can buy a present."

Lauren's face brightened with a glorious smile. "That touches me in a way that I can't describe. Thank you."

Harry shuffled around, and Nicky rushed forward and hugged her friend.

"I guess I need to go and say goodbye to mother."

"Are you going to tell mom that you are leaving, Harry?"

"Great minds, Lauren." Harry chuckled as she tapped a gentle finger on her sister's cheek.

"Yes, I would say so, sis. Nic, may I speak with you for a moment?"

"Of course. Lori, Harry can say her goodbyes without an audience. Don't forget what I said earlier." She grinned at Harry and reaching up, kissed her tenderly.

"Yes, ma'am."

∞

Harry silently opened the door to Victoria's room and disappeared inside.

Inside, Harry saw Steven whispering to his wife. Her mother looked good—marvelous would be a more appropriate description. "Hi, I thought I'd come by and say a proper goodbye. I need to go home."

Victoria looked up at Harry. "I can never begin to tell you how much your coming here has meant to me, Harry. I know it couldn't have been easy for you.

If you're anything like me, you were kicking yourself the whole way." Victoria held her hand out to her daughter. "Is there any way I can be in your life?"

"I think it's too late for that." Harry kicked herself as she realized her mother might misconstrue her words. "Since you already are."

"I love you, Harry. I always have."

"Yes, well, I can't promise it will be all smooth sailing. I don't have my head around the whole scenario yet and I may never completely get there. But, I'm willing to try to get to know you better. It's the best I can offer at the moment."

"What do you say we go slow and see where that takes us?"

"Works for me." Harry smiled in relief at the acceptance that she wasn't going to allow her mother into her life. Who knew what the future might hold? There had been some interesting twists and turns along the way and this diversion had been earth shattering.

Victoria smiled and squeezed her daughter's hand. "Me too." She took a deep breath. "Do you think I could visit you and Nicky?"

Harry hoped the question wouldn't arise just yet; however, now that it had, there really wasn't anything to worry her. The whole mother-daughter situation didn't frighten her anymore as it had previously in her life. She was laying the phantoms to rest. "I think you and Steven could visit. I'll show you my company."

"When you are ready, Harry, we would love to see your company and Houston."

"That's good. Nicky loves to show people around the house we just bought. Do you like gardens?"

"When I was much younger, I had a small flower garden. I called it *Harriet's field*. So, to answer your question, *yes*, I love gardens. I know it sounds strange, but I felt close to you there."

A memory flittered over Harry at the words and she saw in her mind's eye the small area of garden her uncle's gardener had given her when she was six years old. "I had a flower garden once too. I called it *my mother's garden*." Harry was lost for a moment before she shifted out of the old images and shrugged. "Nicky has the green thumb. Mine tends to make flowers die."

"Hey, what do you say I spring for dinner tonight? A farewell of sorts."

"Are you sure you're ready for dinner?"

"Yes, Steve and I were just talking about that very thing before you came in. I was thinking we could commandeer one of the meeting rooms and I will have a dinner brought in for us all. What do you say? Are you game for a little adventure in the culinary delights?"

For some reason, a bubble burst inside Harry at the suggestion and she laughed. "As long as you aren't cooking."

"Darling, I will have you know I do know how to cook. I can boil water and I make a mean tuna sandwich."

"Tuna huh? Maybe one day I'll let you make me one since it's one of my favorites."

Harry winked at Steven who was watching the exchange in happy silence.

"I will hold you to that." Victoria smiled.

"You can. I think this is my cue to leave and settle my bill at the hotel. Nicky and I will see you all later for dinner."

"Great. Is six a good time for you?"

"Perfect. We're leaving at seven in the morning therefore we don't want a late evening."

"What's going on here? Sounds like you two have made plans. Are we included too?"

"I don't know about that little sister, kids aren't allowed at grown up parties you know." Harry chuckled as she cuffed her sister gently under the chin.

"Of course you are, sweetheart." Victoria looked radiant. "Want to have dinner with us tonight?"

"I think I see having an older sister is going to be a challenge." Lauren laughed as the others joined her. "I wouldn't miss this night for anything. Maggie can come too, can't she?"

"Yeah, as long as Nicky can come." Harry relaxed as she felt the warm ambience in the room.

"Try and keep them away." Lauren hugged her sister.

"You take care, little sister. We will see you later." Harry smiled as she released the hug and turned to Nicky who was grinning happily. She stepped closer to Nicky and gently reached out and touched her face. "Let's go, shall we, Nic."

Nicky nodded.

Steven turned to his wife and daughter. "We have all we will ever need in this room and down the hall with Maggie. We have come full circle and it is so very right."

"Amen to that."

"Yes, love has wonderful, curative powers." Victoria watched her daughter leave the room.

∞

The first tentative steps to atonement were forged with compassion, love and understanding. There was still a long way to go, but the assent up the hill had begun. A single tear began the journey through the gentle sunset toward a new beginning that starts with reconciliation

About the Author

JM Dragon

Born in England, JM Dragon is and now a New Zealand citizen, living in the beautiful Canterbury countryside. JM Dragon loves to garden, travel and has a love of animals. Her animals, many of them strays, even the odd chicken, have proved a new focus in her life. Sharing her life with her family, two cats, two alpacas, and over forty Bantam chickens in differing breeds; she's found a totally different focus in her life than when she lived in England.

Her writing is a long cherished release for the characters that invade her mind on many an occasion. Always having written stories from a child, she found the Internet a place she could share her creative world with other readers. Having stumbled across venues on the net for her writing, she found new subjects to explore. She currently loves the creative, readership and friendship genre she has comfortably taken residence in for the last twelve years.

A keen reader of sci-fi, crime/mystery, classic, and romance of course, JM Dragon is here to stay and loves to experiment with storylines – who knows what she will tease us with next.

Erin O'Reilly

First challenged by a friend to write a story, Erin has since written numerous online and publish works. Her story *Deception* was a GCLS Finalist in 2008. That book also garnered the Sapphic Readers Award in 2009. Story creation involving strong characters always seems to dictate the story and invade her mind at all hours. It always amazes here when the characters she is developing suddenly take on a life of their own and lead the story down a completely different path. She thinks that the characters make an impact on the storyline making the story better.

E-Books, Limited First Edition Print, Printed Books,
Free e-books

Visit our website for more publications available
online.

http://www.affinityebooks.com

Published by Affinity E-Book Press NZ Ltd

Canterbury, New Zealand

Registered company 2517228